MW00897686

Schmuck

A novel

By Ryan Spargo

Copyright © 2016 Ryan Spargo

Cover Design © 2016 Ryan Spargo, Leslie Spargo

First Edition 2016

All rights reserved. This book or any portion thereof may not be reproduced or used in any manner whatsoever without the express written permission of the publisher except for the use of brief quotations in a book review or related essay.

The characters contained in this work of fiction are, themselves, a work of fiction and do not represent any particular parties or persons. Any similarities to persons, living or dead, is purely coincidence and is not intentional. I promise. Pinkies, even.

ISBN: 152379402X

ISBN-13: 978-1523794027

DEDICATION

This book is dedicated to my wife. Because of her, no story or tale will ever be good enough, because it will always pale in comparison to ours.

CONTENTS

ACKNOWLEDGMENTS

This book is a dream come true. It's one thing to have a dream that you believe in, but it's another thing entirely to see that dream come to fruition. It's also one thing to believe in your dream alone, but to have people believe in you and support you through it all is something I couldn't possibly have imagined. I always knew I'd have a section of my first book that thanked several people, but I never imagined that section being this long. And trust me when I say that I won't be insulted if you skip this part. I do need to thank a few special people though, and now seems like a great time to do so.

To Leslie, my wife: thank you for loving every bit of my weird, neurotic self. You're my greatest dream come true.

To my sister, Kindle: thank you for being the perfect sister that I never had. You're somehow a treasure and also a treasure hunter. Well done.

To Mom and Dad: thank you for being Top Tier contributors to the I-Promise-I'm-Eventually-Going-To-Be-Someone-Successful fund. Wind beneath my wings and what not.

To Karen and Scott (My perfect in-laws): Karen, for your endless motivational praise and support, and Scott, for indulging me when I told you, "It has to be a .22," even though there are "manlier calibers available."

To Casey, Chris, and Mark: thank you for riffing jokes with me enough to teach me how comedy works.

To Thad: you're an ass, and that has been invaluable in my pursuit to become a writer. I, too, hope this book doesn't suck.

To Jeremy: thanks for being on the other side of the cubicle, always ready to test ideas and get lost in story development.

To Dr. Bill Larsen: thank you for helping me realize how much I love writing. This book would be impossible without you.

To my aunt Kim: thank you for telling a silly, impatient child those wonderful stories during the long hike. You planted the seed far before I even knew there was soil.

To Mary, Irene, Morgan, and Leni: thanks for keeping me sane during our long hours, and thanks for giving me time in the warehouse to draw inspiration. See? Told ya I'd mention you.

Okay, I'm done. Thanks for the opportunity to share my gratitude. Now let's get on with it.

CHAPTER ONE

Benny sat at the edge of his bed, staring at the floor. He wasn't really sure how long he'd been sitting there, but he knew he'd gotten up somewhat early, and the late afternoon, autumn sun was already beginning to set. The room was almost completely silent except for the sound of the A/C running, and that was merely a dull hum. Still, he felt like there was a constant, haunting roar in the room. Sometimes, he'd sit in the other bedroom down the hall just to escape the sound of his own room. He had lately begun to think of it as his panic room, especially since he wasn't using the other half of his two-bedroom apartment for anything else. Despite not having a roommate, Benny had chosen a two-bedroom because it hadn't been that much more expensive than the one-bedroom. *And*, he had thought, *it'll give me a lot more space. Maybe I'll make the other bedroom into an office or a game room.*

But the other room was empty. Benny had been living in his place for a year now, and no one had ever occupied that space. Actually, that's not quite true. Once, he left the window open and a finch flew in. He tried to get the finch out, but when the finch landed in the closet, Benny decided he could stay. "I won't even charge you rent, sir," he had said with a childlike grin. The finch only stayed for a few minutes, and then he flew out just as he had come. Oh, except he left Benny a surprise on the floor that stained the wood.

Benny had no trouble affording the apartment. He worked for a public relations firm located downtown and could make the rent payments very easily. The building was a converted loft at the top of the old Kernley Building. He lived a block from Main Street, and he usually fell asleep to either the sounds of the busy city or whatever old movie was playing on the film channel. In fact, considering his financial security and rising future with a growing Fortune 500 company, and only at the ripe age of twenty-seven, one would think he would feel proud and happy.

But Benny sat there, in his room, alone.

He checked his phone's clock. 3:15 P.M. He put the phone down, but the phone immediately rang. It was Benny's friend Kyle. Kyle was calling him for one reason: he needed a buddy to go drinking with him so that he didn't have to be responsible. Now, Kyle would never say it like that. He'd ask Benny if Benny had any plans, and then Kyle would tell him about this "hot new bar/club/dive/den" that they just had to "hit up tonight," as if the place was handing out actual placards to indicate whether or not one was cool.

Benny sighed. He considered answering. He really did. But then he thought the night through. He would meet Kyle in an hour. They'd start drinking. Girls would show up. He would be nervous and make idle conversation, and the girls would laugh at Kyle's cocky jokes and humor. Kyle was always the ladies' man of the two. Benny had never been much of a charmer, despite being a tall, dark-haired young man with a strong jaw line and a larger, broad frame. In fact, Benny, unbeknown to him, drew the ladies' attention before Kyle, but Kyle's personality won out every time.

Kyle would have too many drinks, and Benny would have to drive Kyle back to Kyle's apartment. They always took Kyle's car so Kyle could drive them to the bar as a show of good faith in his "responsible nature." But, when Kyle was wasted, Benny had to be designated driver, and that meant he would end up driving Kyle home in Kyle's own car. He would then get in his own car and drive home. And there wouldn't be any convenient parking in the garage, so he would have to park at the top and walk down the stairs. And that one section has the burned out bulb, so he would have to walk it blind. And all of this relied on him arriving home by two o'clock in the morning, which he probably wouldn't.

He declined the call and put the phone down. Kyle would leave some voice mail about how Benny was less of a man for not going out with him tonight. He'd probably imply that Benny preferred the company of burly gentlemen as opposed to ladies. He did so every time.

Benny got up to get a drink from the kitchen. He wandered to the refrigerator and opened the door. His refrigerator held nothing but a half-jug of orange juice and a single can of cheap light beer, Kyle's drink of choice. He shut the door and chose tap water. He turned with his glass of water to the empty room. Ironically, Benny had kept the room very tidy despite his lack of attempts to find a roommate. *Maybe I could get a big fern for the room,* he considered. *I could put it in the middle of the room. I could even make a note for the door that reads 'The Jungle Room.'* He chuckled at the idea. He slunk back to his room and sat on the edge of his bed and checked the time, setting the phone back down on his pillow.

As if on schedule, his phone rang. He picked it up but didn't check to see who was calling. He knew immediately. He was prepared. He'd gotten his drink and was seated. No interruptions. The voice on the other end wouldn't want anything distracting him. Karen hated to be interrupted.

Karen was Benny's girlfriend. They had been dating for almost two years, and their anniversary was coming up next week. He met Karen in a local bookstore about three blocks from his firm. She was thumbing through a copy of the latest political commentator's exposé on the flaws of his previous political party affiliation. He thought she looked brilliant, with her raincoat and her hair pulled up in a tight bun.

Benny spent a good ten minutes working up the nerve to say something to her. He finally chose to go with a vague comment on her book, hoping she'd be confused enough to ask what he meant and then become locked in conversation. He walked sheepishly over to her and commented that the book was the best in the series, not even knowing if that particular book was truly the best in the series nor even if there was a series at all. Karen turned and told him she'd consider buying it and come find him later so he could ring her up. Benny started to correct her, and then decided to just let her read.

She found him later crouched in the graphic novels. She told him she was ready to check out. He coughed. "I, um, don't work here." "Oh, I'm sorry. You look like the kind of person who works in a book store." Benny smiled and rose, somehow inspired and amused by her and what he would pretend was a compliment. They spent the next ten minutes talking about how hard it was to find the bathrooms in the store and how poorly the architect had designed the layout.

Benny, seated on his bed, checked his phone. He thought, as he always did when Karen called, that he could just let it go to Voicemail. But Karen hated, hated, HATED Voicemail. She had yelled at him for letting it go to Voicemail once. He thought being at his grandmother's funeral excused him, but Karen thought otherwise. So, he never let it go to Voicemail. He had never even wanted a phone to begin with, but Karen told him, "no self-respecting man goes about in this day and age without a means of communication at all times." He reluctantly agreed, though it seemed like the only reason he had a phone was so she could call. Not wanting to keep her waiting any longer, he hit Send.

"Hello, honey...... yes, I........ right, I went today......... it was nice...... How's Atlanta? Oh, they have you working that much? Well, I suppose it's good for your career. No, I meant......... No, of course. You're right. They shouldn't treat you like that......... of course you deserve that office........ she shouldn't have said that. Yes, she seems like an ass. You're probably right. Oh, okay....... Yes, I'll talk to you soon. I'm going to go out. Yeah, I need some fresh air. No, I'm......... no, I didn't talk to Kyle. He called, but I didn't answer. Right.......

Okay, I'll let you go. Take care. I love you too. Bye." Benny closed his phone and finished his water with a large gulp. He walked to the kitchen, put the glass in the dishwasher, and wandered down the hall.

Passing his bedroom, he walked to the double French doors of the balcony to his apartment. The doors had been a big selling point to the apartment, as they seemed to have that modern uptown air that he had been looking for in an apartment. He loved the sights of the city at night, listening to the traffic cops, the cars, and the sounds of people enjoying the nightlife. But, the balcony had never really been cleaned, and he hated feeling the dirty rails and surfaces, so he had progressively sat on the balcony less and less over time. The only time he had really spent out there was the night of the 4Th of July, but that ended abruptly when his neighbor downstairs started fighting rather loudly with her boyfriend.

He stared out the windows of the balcony doors, looking at the city he knew so well. Normally, it brought him a sense of calm and joy to see the city shining in the passing day's sun, but, for the past few months, things hadn't been the same. He just wasn't enjoying the sights like he once did.

Returning to his room, he sat at the edge of his bed and began thinking. Usually, he did his best thinking at the edge of his bed. Tonight, however, he wasn't thinking about big plans or activities or even the cable schedule. Tonight, Benny was thinking about his miserable life. He was thinking about how he didn't matter. He wasn't thinking about if he mattered at work, or if he mattered to his friends and coworkers. Benny was thinking about how he didn't matter to anyone or anything.

Benny looked at the edge of his bed by the headboard. On the floor, next to the bed and slightly tucked under the bed skirt, sat an old shoe. Benny stooped down and picked it up. He slumped down on the bed and reached into the shoe. Inside, he gripped and removed the .22-caliber pistol he kept inside.

He kept the gun by his bed at all times. He considered it a means of self-defense in the city, and, considering he lived alone, he thought it the best means. He kept it in an old shoe because, at least in his opinion, it was the best gun safe he had. *No one would ever think to look in an old shoe for a gun. It's hidden beneath my bed*, he thought, even though there was no mate for the shoe, and it really didn't even look like it had been worn in years. But, to be fair, it was cheaper than a gun safe.

Benny held the loaded gun timidly. His hands always shook just a little when he held a gun. He probably would never have been able to shoot a single thing, but he liked to think he could be a crack shot in a moment of duress. He'd chosen the small .22 because it was quite lightweight, easy to conceal should he decide to carry it, the ammunition was a little more affordable, and he'd read once in an online article that it was an assassin's weapon of choice due to the lack of exit trajectory of each bullet or something. He had been interested in carrying a concealed firearm, but he had never taken the class and acquired his license. *Those classes are at least $250*, he had marveled at the time, and that seemed like far too much money just for a card that said one could carry a gun legally. He figured that, should a moment ever arise where he needed to shoot someone threatening him, the law would be on his side.

He considered what he was actually thinking of doing. Could he really kill himself? He had never really said that before, but he'd thought it for a few weeks. He had considered what it would mean to the world if he died. He knew the value of human life, mostly because he'd seen *It's a Wonderful Life* so many times. He felt arrogant for wondering if the world would miss him, but then he also felt angry that he didn't feel appreciated by the world.

The thought nagged at Benny. It would be so simple. All he had to do was put the gun to his head and pull the trigger. It would be loud, but what would he care? He would be dead. In fact, someone in his apartment building would probably hear and come running, or, at the very least, call the police. He'd be found, relatives would be notified, friends would gather, a grave would be laid, and he could finally relax. And there would be no damage to the apartment walls, so his family could probably still get the security deposit back.

But then he considered the moment further. Where exactly does one shoot oneself to ensure a kill? *Am I supposed to put the barrel in my mouth? Maybe the side of the head is fine.* He then chose to decide which was best by miming them all. He put the gun in his mouth, making sure not to let his lips or tongue touch the barrel. The gun had been in an old shoe, after all. He put the barrel to the side of his head, and then the front. Then, he tried to put the gun on the back of his head. The gun almost fell out of his hands, and he fumbled to catch it. He was terrified that it would go off if dropped.

A thought occurred to Benny: did he really want to die in this apartment? Is that what he really wanted? Benny considered that, since he lived in the city, there were plenty of "cool" places to die. "I could even curl up in the park and do it there," he said aloud, as if he needed to convince someone else in the room. So, he grabbed his pea coat and scarf and tucked the gun into his coat pocket. He looked around his apartment, presumably for the last time, and stepped into the main hall closing the front door behind him. A moment later, he opened the front door and reentered his room. He grabbed his cell phone from the bed, just in case Karen called. He stepped back into the main hall, closed his front door, and locked it. *One can never be too careful in the city*, he thought.

CHAPTER TWO

Benny walked down the stairs of the apartment lobby and out into the street. The streets were still lit from the fading autumn sun that occasionally shone through the clouds. He liked the whole experience, watching the sun sink behind the horizon of his big city life, but he often reminded himself how little the city actually was. Granted, the downtown district had skyscrapers. Well, at least cloud scrapers. There was a busy market square, and the local theatre even had a big, bright sign that could be seen from both ends of Main Street. He noted that he could see it even from his apartment off Wershuck Avenue. He'd never really considered himself a city-dweller, but he had never once regretted moving into the city. The whole thing made him feel upper class and well-to-do, and yet he knew it was all a charade he used to feel more important.

Benny made sure the pistol was tucked firmly into his coat pocket. He didn't want anyone to see it, for fear he'd be arrested and have to spend the night in some prison cell with the madmen and repeat offenders of the city. He'd seen those crime shows and detective dramas. He knew what kind of men were waiting in lock up. He knew it was called lock up.

The streets were busy with the business men striding to their sedans after a long day at the office, the women shopping in the small stores that lined Main Street, and the families enjoying the weather. He had to smile at the scene. He had always dreamed of being someone important in a big city. Fresh out of college, Benny had landed a job with a prestigious public relations firm about a hundred miles away from his hometown. He had moved three years ago and had found a small one bedroom immediately. But, after being promoted to his current position, Benny took it upon himself to find "a place more suited to his earning level." At least, that's how Karen had described the decision when she talked him into it.

He considered how convenient it was that his firm wasn't open on Wednesdays. The CEO, whom he'd never met but had heard legends of almost every day, hated what he called "Hump Day," and he refused to do business on Wednesdays. He noted how convenient it was that today was "Hump Day." What if he had wanted to kill himself on a Thursday? Maybe this was a sign from the universe that his death was meant to be.

Benny took a moment to look back at his apartment building. He saw Mrs. Meihner on the second floor shaking her rugs out onto the street. From all that cigarette smoke caked in there, it looked like she was making smoke signals to the neighborhood. He saw his own apartment's window by the bedroom. He loved to sit at that window and just stare out into the streets. He always made sure to close it and pull the drapes after eleven o'clock. One could never be too careful at night.

"Hello, Benjamin," Mrs. Meihner called down to him, waving from her smokey perch. "Lovely weather this evening." He really wished that she hadn't seen him. She was a really sweet lady, but he just wasn't in the mood to chat. "Yeah, it's really nice," he replied, unsure of what else to add to the conversation. "Are you going walking?" she asked. "Tonight's a nice night for a walk." He shrugged and said, "I think so. I'm just going to walk around for a while." Mrs. Meihner sighed and put her hands on her hips. "Benjamin, you should go find a nice girl and take her out tonight. See the world, get out a little more. You're too young to stay cooped up in that apartment of yours." "Well a little fresh air never hurt anyone, I suppose. Have a good night, Mrs. Meihner," he said, waving as he turned away. "Good luck, Benjamin," she called down, watching him walk away. As he turned back to wave once more, his foot caught the small lip of the sidewalk, and he tripped a little, stumbling without falling. Mrs. Meihner chuckled to herself, shook her rug once more, and sighed, "What a schmuck." Benny quickened his pace and hurried away before she could say another word.

Benny walked down the streets toward Market Place. The city gave the small shopping center this name because they hoped people would congregate there and make the city look popular. And they were right, people did, but most people used it as the best way to cut through downtown. The sights were always worth the extra block's walk. The rising musicians and talent acts tried their best new material here. It was a free show every day.

Stopping in the middle of the square to sit at a table, Benny regarded the shops. He considered shooting himself in front of one. *Sort of a statement about the over-indulgence of America,* he thought. But then he realized how little he'd actually bought from these shops and how nice some of the items in the windows looked. He decided not to do that. He'd never been much of a protester. Well, except for that time the Harry Potter movies were delayed at his local movie theatre, and he'd stood outside with the crowd shouting, "Bring the magic!" That was the closest he'd been to being an activist.

Benny regarded his decision to end his life. As he often did to solve problems, Benny had an inner conversation with himself. *"Why do it?" "Why not? What have you got to live for?" "Well, I have a good job, a great girlfriend, and a promising career. I just feel lost a lot, like I don't matter." "Do you matter?"* He asked himself this question a lot, and he had hoped that by now he'd know the answer. Yet, after twenty-seven years of living, he still didn't.

He checked the time on his phone. 4:30 PM. He felt in his pocket for the pistol. The smooth metal felt cold against his hand. He only checked it for a moment, not wanting to draw attention to himself.

He looked across the square to the next block. The walking

bridge began there and ran across the main roadway to the park. Benny could see the lampposts of the park still unlit. By the time he walked over there, he knew they'd be lighting. He thought of the park and how fondly he'd loved to watch the children play. Benny envied children. They had no worries, no concerns, and no problems. Their lives were free of burden and duty. They didn't care what the stock market was doing, who was on Twitter, or whom the latest celebrity gossip was trashing. They just wanted to go outside and play. Benny wished for that life again.

He began the walk across the street to the park. As he came to the top of the short steps to the walking bridge, he noted some graffiti on the brick wall to the left. Someone had used a stencil to spray paint the words "Turn off the TV" across the red painted brick. Beneath that, someone had written "Why?" in thick felt permanent marker. A line of retorts lay beneath that in various marker colors: "Because it's killing your mind." "But I'll miss 'Real Ninja Trials'." "When is that on?" "Fridays at 9:30 PM EST."

Benny turned his eyes back to the bridge. He looked across the walk and stared. Benny had always fantasized about having one of those classic movie moments where a hot, young woman passes his way and time stops, a moment where only the two of them mattered, where nothing else in the world existed except the meeting of two souls forever connected. Benny was a romantic, and a hopeless one at that. It was, at that moment, she appeared.

Across the bridge came a young redhead, jogging in time with her mp3 player. Her warm, bright red hair was pulled into a ponytail, despite being no longer than shoulder length. She wore a black runner's jacket with a pink tank top underneath and black yoga pants. Her shoes were black with pink highlights. She was a vision in pink neon accents. Benny froze.

She jogged with her eyes set on the concrete of the bridge. Benny could have sworn that time stood still, but that was simply because the light was red below the bridge, and oncoming traffic had literally stopped. She jogged slowly toward him, and, to

Benny, she hovered and never touched the ground. It was as if she floated just an eighth of an inch off the ground, like an angel trying to disguise her ability to fly. As she approached him, he caught the scent of something sweet and fragrant, and he felt himself becoming intoxicated by the aroma. Her face glistened with tiny beads of sweat in the setting sun, and she seemed to shine. As she passed him, she looked up and saw him. She grinned at him and giggled just slightly, probably because Benny was standing there with his mouth hanging open. She passed, skipping a step at the bottom and stopping at the crossing sign for only a moment before dashing across the street.

Benny stared for a moment longer, watching this angel on Earth jog away from him. He was locked in this gaze until he felt his pocket vibrate. He feared his legs were giving out, and then realized his phone was ringing. He pulled the phone from his pocket and saw Karen's name blazed across the readout. He almost shouted, realizing his girlfriend was calling while he burned holes into another woman with his gaze. He stood for a moment, slowing his breaths, and then answered the call. "Hello hun. Yes.......... What? No..... I....... no I was just walking fast. Yeah, just getting some air...... no I .... yes that's why I'm out of breath. Your call startled me. Are you back at the hotel? Oh good............ Why do you have to room with her? Can't you just......... oh that's terrible........... I know, that's so unfair of them............ you should complain..... no, no, I know you can take care of yourself. I wasn't saying.......... of course honey. No, you're right. She can just deal with it.......... Okay, I'll talk to you soon. Have a good time at dinner........ I love you too....... No, I'm just out for a walk......... exactly. Take care. Bye."

Benny pocketed the phone. His passing angel had already turned the corner. He wanted to call to her. He wanted to see her again, and he wished he knew her name. He had no idea why, but he just thought to himself that, if he knew her name, somehow things would be different. Somehow, his life would be better, if only by a little.

Benny had just reached the bottom of the stairs leading down from the walking bridge and into the park when he was met with a thin ragged man. The man stopped him and, staring into Benny's eyes with a seemingly meaningful look of desperation, said, "Hey man, listen. I'm not gonna feed you a line or a story. I'm not gonna bull you like that. I'm not gonna give you a line, man. But look here, man, I gotta get uptown to my old lady. She sick somethin' bad, and I gotta get a bus ticket. I gotta get just a few dollars more for the ticket. Can you help me out? I hate to ask you like this with you goin' where you're headed, and I'm not feeding you a story or a line, but I gotta get some dollars for the bus to help my sick old lady." The man then held out his hand, as if this was the part where Benny emptied his wallet into the man's waiting hands.

Benny was a patient and understanding man, and he secretly prided himself on being kind and giving. He'd never turned a blind eye to those in need. Okay, well, he'd never avoided giving a dollar. He'd certainly never let someone into his apartment, but he tried to always be kind and supportive. So why was it that, here in this moment, he wanted to shoot this guy in the head? Didn't this guy understand how miserable Benny was? Couldn't he see how much Benny's life sucked and how Benny was trying to end it all? He hadn't asked anyone for help at all, and yet this man couldn't scrounge together a few measly dollars for bus fare. Benny told the man he couldn't help and brushed past him. The man called over Benny's shoulder, "Man, thanks anyways. Good luck gettin' where you gotta go."

Benny made three laps around the park, trying his best to calm his nerves. He was surprised that, in that time, he hadn't run into the guy asking for money again. Maybe that guy really did need money and Benny didn't help him. Shaking himself from the guilt that had begun to fester, he took a deep breath and let it out slowly. Benny knew what he had to do. He began to search the park, looking for a place to make his peace. He saw an awning and thought it perfect. But there were children still playing. He couldn't just shoot himself here in front of them. What if he scarred them for life?

Making another loop, Benny saw the rocky base of the nearby waterfall. The city had installed a small waterfall that fed into the lower stream of the pond/tiny lake/whatever-kind-of-body-of-water-it-was that sat in the middle of the park's main way. The rocks had clearly been colored to look as if moss and lichen naturally grew there, and yet there was a distinct scent of chlorine in the misty air around the falls. *The thing looks like a rock garden pond that people put in their yards to seem fancy,* he jeered to himself.

He considered shooting himself there. His body might just fall to the bottom of the pond water. *Oh, maybe it wouldn't be found for a few days. The police might consider it fowl play and try to find the killer,* Benny mused. He smiled at this, loving the idea of him becoming the "innocent victim" in an "ongoing murder investigation." He really did watch a lot of cop dramas. But then he considered what the odds were of the police making his case a citywide mystery. They'd probably just regard it as one of those park murders that happen without rhyme or reason and close the case. Benny then thought of his family, what little family he still had in his life. How would his poor aunt deal with the idea of him being murdered? How could she handle the grief? It would probably be easier to know he'd just killed himself. *No one to blame but me,* he thought with a sigh.

I need to go sit in my spot and think this through, Benny thought. Benny's "spot" was a medium-sized oak tree that sat at one edge of the park in a secluded run of trees and bushes. He loved to sit there and just think. He never thought about anything in particular. He liked it because it was so cut off from the rest of the park. No one came back there, except the occasional dog walker looking for a bathroom on the go. He could hide away from the world there, and he could spend as long as he want—

Benny laughed for not thinking of it sooner. His favorite spot was perfect. He could lay there in peace and be found the next day by the park security. All he had to do was find a nice patch of dirt where he could cozy up and shoot himself. He walked to the clearing he knew so well and stood surveying the scene.

It was perfect. The leaves were falling, and hopefully some would fall on Benny as he lay there. It was almost poetic. Benny smiled and crossed his arms, delighting in his accomplishment. This would be his crime scene. Benny looked the tree over. There wasn't really a good place to hide and have peace. The bushes at the base, however, were full and low. He could tuck into one and end it there. He'd still be visible, but only if someone looked for more than a moment.

He crouched by an average-sized shrub. *This is a good bushy bush. I could do it here.* Circling around the tree, he checked the mulch for dog poop. He didn't want to lay in it, after all. *What kind of man chooses to shoot himself and lays down in dog crap?* Not Benny. He had more self-respect than that.

Benny dusted the loose mulch away and lay down sideways. He immediately felt the cold of the mulch and wished he'd picked a warmer day to do this. He had to raise himself up slightly and pull the gun from his pocket. In his rush, he'd forgotten to take the gun out. He took a few deep breaths and considered where to shoot himself. Through the heart? That might not kill him. Through the head? This has to end it all. He didn't want to suffer. Benny was ashamed at how little he'd thought about this since he walked over here. Once again, Benny hadn't managed his time well. Benny decided the heart was best. It was poetic and romantic. He could just see the paper headlines talking about the young bright man who "broke his own heart." He hoped they'd use that line.

Benny sighed. This was it. He was ready. It was time to do what he came to do. Benny felt to make sure the clip was in. He laughed, thinking that he really should have done that before he left the apartment, but thankfully the gun was loaded. After checking the gun over twice, he steadied his hand as best he could. This was it. He was ready.

Benny put the gun's barrel to his chest. He took some breaths to ready himself. He closed his eyes and prayed one last prayer. He prayed for strength for his family. He prayed for his family's safety. He prayed for many things. Then, he realized he hadn't prayed for Karen. He prayed for Karen's… he prayed… Benny didn't really know what to pray for concerning Karen. In the end, he prayed for Karen by saying he hoped she was happy. With that, Benny resigned himself to his fate. Wrapping his hand tightly around the grip of the gun, Benny eased his finger onto the trigger and waited for the inevitable shock.

CHAPTER THREE

The park was quiet. The wind whistled through the branches of the trees and down across the grass, as if to lead anyone near by to the still body of a young man in a pea coat and jeans. Benny lay silent, his body slumped against the crushed leaves beneath the tree.

Well, not completely silent. The faint rattle of metal could be heard. Slowly, he opened his eyes, wondering from where the sound was coming. He soon realized that the sound was coming from his pistol, clutched tightly in his trembling hand. The shaking pistol had not fired as he believed, for he had never pulled the trigger. Instead, Benny had simply squeezed the grip of the gun so tightly that his hand was turning red.

He eased his grip and sighed. *What the hell am I doing? This isn't right,* he thought to himself. He relaxed, falling backward onto the ground and kicking leaves up around him. He felt his head hit the mulch beneath the tree, and, for a single moment, he realized he probably had mulch in his hair. Benny sighed, admitting to himself that he just didn't care.

He wasn't sure how long he had lain there like that, but eventually, he became aware of a small creature that was breathing very close to him. Slowly, he opened one eye to reveal a small blond-headed boy of maybe six or seven years old standing close to him, staring at him.

"Hi there," Benny finally said.

"Hi. Are you dead?"

Benny chuckled. "Actually, no."

"You look dead. Or sick. Are you sick?"

"No, I'm not sick." Benny sat up in the leaves. "I'm Benny. Where are your parents?" As if by command, he heard a voice from behind the trees across the small opening yelling.

"I hear your mom yelling for you."

"What are you doing back here, mister?"

Benny paused. "I'm thinking."

"'Bout what?"

"I'm thinking about whether or not I'm happy. I'm wondering about my life." He could see that the child didn't understand what he was saying. "Grown up stuff. Just being weird, I guess."

Benny became aware in that moment that he was still holding the gun. Thankfully, his coat had fallen open onto it, so there was a good chance that the boy hadn't seen the pistol. He eased the pistol back into his pocket.

"My momma says that happy is what you make it. She says I should always be happy to be alive."

Benny smiled, "Well, your mom sounds like she's smart."

"'Scuse me."

Benny paused, looking at the boy.

"'Scuse me."

"Um, what?"

"I said, 'Scuse me.'"

"Oh, um… okay. Why?"

"I pooted. Momma says that I always need to say 'Scuse me' when I poot."

"Oh. Okay. Um… you're excused."

The boy grinned and dashed away to his calling mother. Benny watched him run, wondering if that boy would ever feel like he did. He wondered if there had ever been a time that he could have avoided this. In a strange way, he wanted to warn the boy about life, about the things that would happen to him and the emptiness he might feel some day.

Benny sat there, listening to the wind and the sounds of children playing. He sighed, wishing he fit into this world, wishing that he knew where or how he belonged. But he'd decided one thing was for certain: he wasn't going to kill himself in the park. This place was too beautiful to be stained with his death. *This park deserves better than my pathetic, useless life's end.*

He stood, wiping the mulch from his coat and jeans. He checked his pocket for the gun, and then he made his way back to the stair set leading to the bridge. If he was going to kill himself anywhere, it should be somewhere dark and secluded. Benny didn't want anyone having to bear the burden of seeing him dead, especially a child.

As he climbed the stairs, Benny noted that he didn't see the homeless man from before. He found himself wishing that the man had still been there. Benny didn't really want to talk to him, but he also didn't really want to be alone. He wanted to give the man some money, partially because he felt guilty but mostly because he wanted to feel like he'd made a difference in someone's life. He didn't even really care if the man spent it on booze. The feeling would have still been worth it, as if giving the man a few dollars meant buying purpose to his existence.

Benny also found himself wishing the jogging girl was there, waiting for him at the top of the stairs. He wasn't sure why, but there was just something about her. He kept thinking of her and how she looked so natural, so free, and so genuine. *Why do I care? I have a girlfriend who loves me and cares for me. The last thing I need is to give that up for some woman I don't even know,* Benny scoffed to himself. Karen was a good girlfriend to him, at least most of the time, and Benny was happy with Karen. Or at least he thought he was. Wasn't he? He had never been a very good boyfriend. His relationships were always short lived, and they usually ended with him getting dumped for being weird. Every girl had used that word: "weird." Benny apparently always hit a wall where he suddenly became "weird," and that was something no woman wanted. He had always wondered why his exes called him "weird" right around the time that he began to feel "used." He'd never use that word with them, though. He didn't want to hurt their feelings.

The city was beginning to come alive with the evening air. Benny always marveled at how people came out to do things on Wednesdays, especially since the crowds died out by eleven o'clock. He wondered if it had been a ploy of the local bar owners to try to drive up business for the middle of the week. Kyle often talked about Wednesdays, always commenting that that was "Ladies' night." According to him, "ladies drink for cheap at most places on Wednesdays. That's when the gettin' is good." Benny could never understand the idea of going out drinking on a Wednesday, but then Benny never went out drinking (unless, of course, Kyle called him).

The small city, despite being a kind of sham metropolis, still had quaint charm and class. The city had become a conglomeration of classic boomtown architecture with the new styles and stores of today's generation. Benny enjoyed the romanticism of it all. At least, he assumed it was romanticism. He had never really understood what romanticism really meant. It seemed like a word that one could just throw on any subject and make it more endearing or timeless. The old theatre, The Entertainer, still had most of the original signage and exterior from its glory days. The lights had been refitted with energy saving bulbs that lasted longer, but the effect was still the same. On any given night, especially a cloudy or dark one, the street was almost glowing from the light of the theatre's signs alone. Benny loved going to that theatre, especially when they were showing classic films. The owner loved to play old Cary Grant pictures, and he often nodded to Benny whenever he came to see the shows. Benny appreciated the owner's noticing of his patronage, and he felt himself a VIP of the theatre. He rarely felt important anywhere, so it was nice to be treated that way once in a while. Often, he wondered if he would think so highly of the theatre without that treatment.

Down the street from the old theatre stood the new theatre,

the one that Grand Max Cinemas had created. Benny chuckled to himself every time he saw the two in the street. The new theatre played all the latest blockbusters and upcoming movies, while the old theatre covered concerts and old movie showings for nostalgic customers. This new place, Silver Cineplex 7, quickly became the popular hangout for most young couples in the city. It was the closest theatre in town that wasn't located in a mall, and the atmosphere couldn't have been better for the "big city movie-goers." The local news called them that. He could never tell if that was a tongue-in-cheek joke or if the news crew actually thought that this town counted as a big city.

He turned up the street and headed toward The Entertainer. He always liked to look in and see what was playing. The electric banner on the outside read, "The Apartment. 8 PM." Benny knew the movie well. It was one of his favorites. He sympathized with Jack Lemmon's character: a young man in a big company letting others walk all over him while trying to win the affections of the pretty girl in his office. Except there was no pretty girl in Benny's office whose heart he was trying to steal. He had Karen, and thus he didn't need to steal any one's heart.

So why did Benny wish he could? Why did he dream of meeting that wild, untamed beauty and chasing her to the end of the world? Why was he still thinking about the jogger on the bridge by the park? She wasn't even someone he knew. She could be a drug addict for all he knew. Or maybe she's a call girl. Benny grinned a little and shook her from his mind, laughing at himself for being so predictable. He would get an idea, a person, or even just a simple moment's notion in his head, and his imagination would run off full steam until he gathered himself and brought everything back into reality.

Benny checked his phone again, hoping he had missed a text or call or something that would distract him. The time read "5:30 PM." He looked up at the electric banner. He could make this showing. Maybe that's what he needed. He could go see one of his favorite movies one last time before killing himself. Perhaps it would even be poetic. The movie ends, the credits roll, and then Benny shoots himself in the theatre right there. He considered the thought for a moment, but noted that he had always loved the theatre. Would it not be disrespectful to kill himself in such a sacred place? What would the other patrons think? They'd be mortified. He couldn't do that. He loved the theatre too much to tarnish it with such a horrible act. Benny thought of all the times he'd seen news stories about shootings in theatres. He'd never believed in capital punishment and the death sentence, but, if he had to pick a crime that warranted such a sentencing, a shooting in a theatre would probably be his pick. Benny shrugged his shoulders and walked down the block. He wasn't really even in the mood for a movie anyway.

Soon, he realized he was wandering. He wasn't heading anywhere in particular. He was just walking to avoid the truth: he was lost. And he wasn't lost in the city. He was lost in life. Benny wasn't really sure he'd ever even known where he was going. All his life, everything had been laid out. His family had told him where to go to school, his ex-girlfriends had told him what to wear, and now his girlfriend told him where to live. He had never really had to make decisions. In a way, Benny hadn't ever *lived* his life. He had simply been there to see it happen.

I need something to take my mind off of this, Benny mused. *Have I even eaten today?* He decided to stroll through Market Place and see what struck his fancy. He turned down Richman Boulevard and stopped at the traffic light. He looked both ways, looked both ways again, realized how silly it seemed to avoid being hit by a car when he wanted to kill himself, and crossed the street.

Market Place stood in the heart of the downtown area. It was a kind of retro/vintage/new age breeding ground. Shops, restaurants, art houses, and sweet shops lined the square. The City Board of Tourism had debated calling the area Market Square, but they chose not to as the area wasn't in the shape of a square. It was actually a rectangle, and they feared that people wouldn't like being misinformed. So, instead, they decided on the politically correct name Market Place. There would be no confusion with a name like that.

As Benny walked around Market Place, he considered the people there. He wandered how many of them felt like he did. Did they all have purpose? Why did they all seem so well collected and driven? Did everyone have a purpose there except for him? He began to wonder what being collected and driven even looked like. Was it something that one could see in someone? Maybe people didn't have it together like he thought, but then why did everyone seem to have a reason for going on? Every person around him looked like they knew exactly what they were doing for the rest of the day and maybe even the rest of their lives. When exactly was he supposed to start looking and feeling like that?

Benny was just about to check his phone to see if Karen had called when he heard his name called out from behind. He turned to find a pint glass held in the air towards him, as if someone was toasting to his misery. He followed the arm holding the glass down, and his eyes met on the rounded, stout face of his "friend" Kyle. Benny suddenly became very aware that he had nowhere to hide.

"Bro! What's up, man! I called you earlier, but you must-a been busy. What brings you out and about downtown?" Kyle belted, despite Benny being less than twenty feet from him. Benny resigned to his fate and walked to Kyle's table. Kyle was sitting at an outdoor table of his favorite new downtown bar. He looked like he owned the place, even though Kyle barely made enough to support his drinking habit.

"Yeah, I missed your call earlier. Sorry. I figured you were at work." Kyle laughed, "No way man! I asked off early for this. I've been waiting for this place to open for two weeks, remember?" "Oh yep, now that I think about it, you did mention it to me." Kyle had mentioned the opening to Benny every day. He mentioned it so much that Benny had tuned the entire conversation out, as well as subsequent mentions of the event. Kyle could have added that his grandmother had turned into an armadillo, and Benny would have simply nodded and smiled in blind agreement.

"Nice one, dude. Way to ignore me." Kyle said this as if hurt, but his smile was still glued wide. "So, what are you doing downtown?" Benny searched for a reason to be out tonight, but a good enough reason that he couldn't meet up with Kyle. "Oh just getting some fresh air. I'm not feeling very well, so I was just having a night in." "Huh. Probably a good idea, man. You don't look so hot, especially in the face. Of course, that's how your face looks all the time. Boom!" Kyle pounded his glass on the table at this and grinned, suggesting that Benny had been disgraced by his jab and that his family honor was at stake. "You got me, buddy. Burned me good with that one." "That's how I roll, man. I'm amazing like that." Kyle lifted his arms and placed his hands behind his head.

Normally, Benny would try to pitch an insult or jab back at Kyle. He'd search for something to retort, but it wouldn't really be an insult. It would just be a mindless shout or grunt of something that barely even made contextual sense. Once, he actually "burned" Kyle with a great insult. He was allowed to bring it up for about a week before Kyle said it had to be retired.

But Benny didn't retort. He didn't even try. "Sorry man, I'm just not feeling too great. I'm going to go home." He didn't try to mention he would talk to Kyle later, because he didn't want to lie to Kyle. Benny was always a man of his word. Well, most of the time.

"Ha, okay, man. Go home and relax. You probably need to recharge your manhood," Kyle jabbed, snickering over the rim of his beer glass. Benny sighed and forced a grin. "Yeah, you're right. I'll go home and try to be less womanly," he sighed. Benny wanted this conversation to end soon. He turned to leave, accepting that Kyle was nothing but an interruption in his day. Kyle raised a toast to Benny's back and laughed. "Good luck man. We all have our days. Don't go shootin' yourself or anything."

Benny stopped. Something inside him began to burn. He couldn't move. Was he going to cry? No, that wasn't it. This was anger. Benny was angry. Really, really angry. He felt himself turning back to Kyle. He could imagine his eyes were white hot. In a way, Benny was outside himself. He could see his hands clenching together, his teeth gritting, and his hairs standing at attention. He walked to Kyle's table, stared down at his friend, and felt the fire burn inside him.

"Who do you think you are? You call me, you invite me out, but do you really know me? Have you ever asked about my life with any sincerity? Have you ever actually given a damn about me for more than a convenient cab service? Am I nothing but a ride home for you when you've reached the lowest drunken point in your conquest to get laid? What if I did kill myself today? What would you say? Would you feel remorse? Would you come to my funeral and joke about my manhood or mock my family for raising a supposed 'girl?' Why the hell do I even call you my friend?"

Benny stood there, waiting for Kyle to respond. Kyle stared at him, but the look on Kyle's face seemed as if Kyle was still waiting for Benny to do something. Benny realized that, in his rage and anger, he hadn't actually said those words. He had just thought them in a flash in his head. He hadn't even moved closer to Kyle. Instead, he had just stood there, saying nothing. "Uh, you okay dude?" Kyle asked. "No, Kyle," Benny muttered. "No, I am not." He turned and walked away angrily. As he thrust his hands into his pickets, his fingers rammed against the cold metal of the pistol. Benny couldn't decide if feeling the gun in his pocket made him feel better or worse.

"Nothing sounds good to me. I need something to cheer me up," Benny grunted, once again talking to himself. He walked around the corner of Market Place, and his eyes fell upon the newest treat shop in the area: Lee's Freeze. Lee, the owner, had opened a frozen yogurt shop, a growing pop trend in cities looking to draw the younger crowds. Lee had hoped to be unique by making his own flavor choices available every two weeks, so patrons were always guaranteed to have strong, wild flavors on the menu. Benny had to assume that Lee was rich by now, because the place was packed all day on the weekends.

Tonight, the crowd was relatively tame. A few moms and their kids graced the parlor. Benny decided he needed a sweet treat to cheer himself up. He opened the door and immediately noted that the shop was far warmer inside than the outdoor air. The place had been painted with bright, lively colors, and the whole thing kind of looked like a playpen, which was a good choice considering how many kids and "kids at heart" Lee served a day. Patrons stood at the machines, waiting on their turn to sample the new flavors and fill their cups. Children weaved in and out of their parents' legs, grinning ear to ear.

Benny casually strolled across the room, heading to the cups. He reached toward the smaller stack, fumbling and trying to separate two cups. "Could I please have the other cup?" a voice called from behind him. He finally loosened the two cups, turned to present the other cup, and looked straight into the smiling face of the jogging beauty from the bridge.

CHAPTER FOUR

Benny stood, frozen in place, with two empty vessels of frozen yogurt. Here before him stood the woman who had infected his brain since he first saw her. *Benny, you idiot, she's talking to you. Do something. Say something. For God's sake, man, don't be an imbecile.* The girl grinned and said, "Um... how about that cup?" He looked down at his hand, back at her, grinned and said, "Oh, yeah, sorry. Just couldn't let her go. She's a beauty." He continued to smile and then realized that he still hadn't done anything, so he passed her the cup.

The girl laughed, albeit with a hint of unease. Benny was dumbfounded. *Did I just quickly come up with something borderline charming and witty to say? Did I just respond without stammering and drooling everywhere?* He had never, ever done this. In all his years, Benny had never quickly come up with something anywhere in the neighborhood of "clever" or "charming" or even "amusing" to say to a woman. Benny was lucky if he could tell her where he lived or the color of the coat he was wearing. Benny just wasn't "that guy." He was the kind of guy women forgot about moments after meeting.

Once, in an ATM line, Benny was standing behind a young woman. He had noticed her as he approached the ATM, and he couldn't help but gaze upon her beautiful hair and face. As the line moved ever so slowly toward the machine, Benny searched for the right thing to say to her. He didn't know her name, had no idea what she was like, but he couldn't pass up the chance to say something to a beautiful woman. Destiny could be standing right in front of him, and he simply couldn't let it slip by. So, in a moment of duress and hurried thought, Benny, without saying hello first, uttered, "Man, these lines. They'll stress you out." The woman turned to see Benny was speaking to her and muttered, "Ha, yeah." Benny then continued: "Sometimes you just want to run up to the machine, bash it in, and take the money. Just take it all and run. That'd be cool." The woman's eyes widened, and she gave a small polite grin of "Oh God, he's one of 'those' people," and turned back to the ATM. Never before had Benny seen anyone operate an ATM as fast as she did when she reached the end of the line. Then, she quickly power walked away.

Knowing all this, Benny couldn't help but marvel at how well he seemed to be doing in this new conversation with this beautiful woman. She looked at her cup and said, "Huh, I guess it is a pretty good model. You don't see a lot of these around anymore." Benny chuckled and said, "Well they have to phase out the old models to make way for the future. The froyo biz is a fast and dangerous game." *Seriously, who the hell has taken over my body and is speaking for me? Why isn't this girl finding a place to hide?*

Benny didn't want to seem like a predator, so he turned back to the pumps and began to choose his flavor. There were so many choices, and one could always mix flavors to create another iteration of frozen treat. He liked the options and choices. In a silly way, this gave him power. He could make anything he wanted, eat anything he wanted. Karen and he would often come to Lee's and get a cup of frozen yogurt, but Karen always got one flavor and added maybe one topping from the Toppings Bar. He used to tease her that she was boring, but Karen always dismissed the joke by saying she didn't want her frozen yogurt mixed with a bunch of nonsense and junk food. He often mixed different things into his frozen yogurt to make, what he considered to be, original dishes. He knew very well how silly it might seem, but he relished any chance to be a little "wild and dangerous."

"What do you think you'll get?" the girl asked. He eyed the pumps and responded, "I'm not sure. I don't know what I feel like. I might make a PB&J." "A peanut butter and jelly sandwich?" she quizzed. "You can make that?" "Oh yeah, it's easy," Benny chirped. "All you have to do is this." With that, he dashed over to the Toppings Bar. "One scoop of graham cracker crumbs, evenly on the base," he said, as he shook the scoop of crumbs into the bottom of his cup. Returning to the pumps, he continued: "Next, get a sample of the cake batter flavor, and then add the peanut butter flavor. Then, grab some of the strawberry." He slid back to the Toppings Bar. "Make sure you add some of this raspberry topping," he added, squeezing a bottle of fruit spread onto the mound of yogurt. "From there, add a little more cake batter to the mix. Then, top it all off with a small bit of the crumbs again." Benny shook the last little bit of the graham cracker crumbs onto the top. "There," he said, trying not to look eager and excited. "It's done. Now, the best way to eat this is to dip your spoon in and get each layer without mixing or stirring." Benny took a spoon from the plastic bin and dipped it into the cup. The girl, smirking with disbelief, pulled the spoon from the mound and, twirling it to keep from spilling any, delicately placed the frozen lump in her mouth.

Benny had made this dish before, and, truth be told, it was his favorite. He didn't get to share his creations very often, as he either ate alone or with Karen. Karen never liked anything he made or concocted. He often wished she would be impressed with his ability. Come to think of it, Benny often wished she would be impressed with anything he could do, not that he had many talents. The girl chewed gently, rolling her eyes off to the side as if considering the taste in her mouth. She stopped chewing abruptly, turned her eyes back to him, widened her gaze, and said, "Oh my God, this is fantastic. This tastes just like a PB&J."

Benny felt his pulse race. It had been a very long time since anyone had ever called anything Benny had done or created anything other than "good" or "okay." He couldn't think of a single time anyone had ever used the word "fantastic." He tried his best to look calm and at ease, but he was sure his grin was wider than the walls in the shop.

"Seriously," she continued. "This is so good. I can't believe how much this tastes like a peanut butter and jelly sandwich." Benny laughed, "Hey, we have to pay for that still." She stopped herself from enjoying another bite and set the cup down on the scale. He filled his cup quickly with cake batter, Oreo chunks, and hot fudge. He set his down next to hers. The clerk asked, "Are these together?" He quickly chimed in, "Yes." "No, you don't have to do that," the girl chimed in, but Benny put out a hand. "No, I insist. You complimented my work, and I'll gladly pay for that." He handed the clerk a twenty-dollar-bill and dropped the change returned to him in the tip jar.

Turning to the girl, he handed her the cup of frozen yogurt. "Thank you. You didn't have to do that," she teased. Benny smiled, "I was glad to. Thanks for letting me." The two moved away from the counter and stood for a moment, enjoying spoonfuls of their treats. "What did you make for yourself?" she asked. "Oh, this isn't much," he replied. "I felt like something rich, so I made a chocolate covered Oreo." "Do you always come to this froyo shop and woo the ladies with your chef skills?" Benny almost choked on his treat. Was he really being that obvious? She probably thought he was a creep. "I uh… don't normally eat here with anyone," he finally muttered. She laughed, "I don't believe that. I bet you wait around here just to buy froyo for unsuspecting ladies, wow them with your skills, and then take them off to your sex dungeon." Benny realized he was lightly sweating. He quickly chimed in, "I don't have a sex dungeon. I have a two-bedroom apartment." "Ah ha, see? Already trying to invite me back to your apartment," she said, raising her eyebrows at him with a suspicious gaze.

Benny was mortified. He should have known not to act so weird. *God, I'm surprised she hasn't called the police yet. She's probably a snitch or something against predators and molesters. This is a sting operation.* He should have seen this coming, what with all the specials on TV he'd seen. He should have seen the signs, the tells of a set up.

These sting operations happened all the time, and he was about to be stuffed into a chair and asked a series of embarrassing questions. Someone would show a video of his ATM incident, and then he'd have to explain what his intentions were with this girl in this particular frozen yogurt shop.

The girl burst out laughing. "Man, you are really fun to tease. Lighten up, guy, I'm just kidding." She punched him in the shoulder, and he coughed out a laugh, realizing he'd overreacted. "My name's Becca," she said, sticking a hand out to receive a shake. He put his hand to hers, briefly passing his coat to make sure it wasn't sweaty. "I'm Benny." "Benny, huh? Well it's a pleasure to meet you. Let's sit down. I've been running for a while, and my legs are a little sore." "Okay," he said, moving to allow her to sit first. They sat down in a pair of borderline ugly cloth chairs by the front door. "You were keeping quite a pace earlier." She looked at him, then a spark of memory flashed across her eyes. "Oh yes! You're the guy who was standing by the bridge. I was wondering why you looked familiar. You'd think I'd remember your face, considering how you were staring at me."

Benny turned red, feeling the heat rising in his face. He had never had this happen before. Normally, he lived with the assurance that he would never see an attractive woman again after noticing her in public. He often would fantasize about making conversation and stealing her heart, but except for a short list of particularly uneventful and rather humiliating encounters, he never made a single move towards conversation. He wasn't a brave man when it came to romance. Maybe he had never been brave about anything.

Turning his eyes towards the ground, he casually muttered, "Oh, yeah. That's me. The bridge gazer." Becca smiled and laughed, "Actually, I was flattered. It's hard to feel attractive when you've been running, sweating, and breathing like you're going to die." Becca took another bite of her frozen yogurt. "Damn this is good. This is really good." Benny turned his gaze from the floor. "I was worried I'd seemed weird." "Oh don't worry, you did, but in a cute way. You're cute weird," Becca grinned, helping herself to another bite. There was a new one: cute weird. Benny had never been called cute and weird at the same time before. He couldn't even think of the last time he'd been called cute.

"So," Benny quickly barked, looking to change the subject, "your name, Becca, it's unique. Is it short for anything?" Becca nodded, raising a finger to excuse herself for having taken too large a bite of yogurt. "Ha, yeah, it's a little odd. My parents named me Rebbeccany." Benny must have performed an exaggerated double-take at this, because Becca choked a laugh at seeing his face. "Rebbeccany? Really?" he puzzled. "Yeah, they overheard the name once and thought it was beautiful. Personally, it's been a nightmare. Try explaining to anyone why you're not simply named Rebbecca. I get it all the time. It's much easier to be called Becca. I prefer it anyway," she said, shaking a hand as if to dismiss her proper name. Benny grinned ever so slightly and said, "I happen to think it's quite a lovely name." She smiled, and her cheeks gained a hint of red. *Again with the charming?* Benny laughed to himself. *This must surely be a record for me.*

Becca set her cup down and fanned her face. "God it's hot in here. I mean, sure, crank the heat up in an ice cream shop, but still," she sighed. "I need to get this fleece off. "I was hoping you'd say something. I'm burning up in this coat," Benny said, tugging at one sleeve. Becca reached back and pulled the hair tie holding her hair up. Her bright red hair fell down her face, lashing at her smoky green eyes and resting just above her shoulders. Benny lost hold of the sleeve he was tugging and blindly pawed after it, unable to look away. Unzipping her black fleece, she pulled the panels back, revealing her bare shoulders. In what seemed like a single, swift motion, she pulled the fleece off her right arm and down her left, casually gathering the bundle into her lap. Benny was definitely staring now.

She was certainly beautiful, but seeing her now took his breath away. Becca's full-figured frame was decorated by a pink tank top that accentuated every curve and line of her body, as if the two were made from the same mold. Her hips, her breasts, her stomach: every square inch of her body seemed a work of art, right down to the patches of freckles cascading down her arms. Benny had seen many beautiful women in his life, but there was no doubt in his mind that he was witnessing a truly unique sight. It seemed like minutes since she had removed her fleece, yet in reality it had been seconds. As Becca turned her head back to him, he became aware that he was ogling. Hell, he was bordering on drooling, and he was frankly embarrassed. Benny had also accomplished the task of getting half his coat off, but the other half was still glued to him.

She turned, caught him in the frozen act of staring, and burst out laughing. "You okay there, Benny? Need some help?" she teased. Benny, coming to his senses, tripped over the words "No, I, no" and "Just let me, uh." He finally got his last arm out and folded his coat over the back of the chair. Gathering his composure, he turned back to Becca who had, too, regained her composure after stifling her laughing fit. "Well that's much better," she said, smiling at him. He couldn't be certain, but he would almost swear that she ran her eyes briefly over his chest. Benny decided to believe that she did, and he made a mental note to purchase more colors and pairs of this particular shirt.
It was then that Benny suddenly realized he wasn't miserable. In just the short time he'd been sitting with Becca, he had forgotten his woes and misery from earlier. Was he simply just depressed and needed something new in his life? Or was she special? Was she something more than just a distraction from his misery? He found himself thinking about living on, seeing more of life, and maybe seeing more of Becca. But that was absurd. He had a woman in his life. He had Karen, and they were happy together. They had been happy together for a while. *Right,* Benny thought to himself. *We're happy, aren't we? Of course I'm happy with her. Aren't I?*

Becca, digging back into her yogurt, broke the silence. "So, Benny, that's an interesting name. You don't seem like a Benny." He shook off his mind's maze and said, "Oh, yes. It's a family name. My father was a Benjamin, and so were both of my grandfathers." "Hmm, that's quite a lot of similar names. I bet family functions were a nightmare," she said with a mouth full of yogurt. He laughed, "When I was younger, my parents called me Benny to keep from confusing me. Benny just sort of stuck. I've been Benny ever since." She set her cup down and rubbed her chin. "Nope, I just don't see it. You're much more of a Ben than a Benny." Ben. No one had ever called Benny that. Oddly enough, that was the name he preferred. He had become so used to "Benny" that he never brought it up.

"So, Ben," Becca piped up, setting her empty yogurt cup down, "what do you do for a living?" "I'm a PR Consultant for Martin and Glowrey," he said, giving little significance to the firm name. She raised her eyebrows, "Woah, that's a pretty good gig. They're quite a name in town. I bet you bring home the big bucks for that." He chuckled, because the truth was he really did. The job had arguably the best pay anyone could ask for at twenty-seven, and Benny worked very hard for the firm. He had been saving his money for quite some time, but he still lived comfortably and spent more than he really should.

"It's a good job," he replied, "and the work is really fun." He started to take one last bite of his yogurt, but he stopped. Dropping the spoon into the cup, he set it down on the table next to them. "That's a lie. It's not fun. I hate my job." Becca's smile faded from her face. He leaned forward, resting his arms on his legs. "I've hated my job for a while now. I don't know when it happened, but the magic just kind of disappeared. I've just grown tired of the whole thing." "That sucks. I'm sorry, Ben. Did something happen to you at work?" she asked, moving a little closer to him. "No, not really, and that's kind of the point. Every day is the same. I come in, I browse accounts, I make phone calls, I schedule events and promotions, I chat with coworkers about the same subjects as the day before, and I go home. It's the same thing every day. I'm not exactly sure, but I think I'm dead inside." He shuffled his feet and slumped back into the chair.

Becca stood and grabbed the two yogurt cups. She tossed them into the garbage cans by the door and returned to her chair.

Putting her fleece on, she said, "Come on, let's go for a walk. You could use it." He smiled and stood, slipping his coat on much more gracefully than when he had removed it. The two turned and walked out the front door of the shop, turning right. "Where to?" He asked, turning to his new friend. Becca had turned her attention elsewhere, looking across the street. She seemed to be focusing on something, as if that something surprised her. After a small pause, she turned back to him and smiled. "Charm me, Mr. Big Shot. Take me somewhere bright and colorful." "Ha, I'll do my best, though I don't know where to take you that you haven't been or seen already," he laughed, motioning for her to join him. She skipped to his side, wrapping her arm around his. "Lead on," she grinned.

The two walked down the street making casual conversation. As they reached the corner and turned, a dark grey van started its engine. The passenger motioned forward, and the driver pulled out into the street, slowly creeping down the avenue and leaving the headlights turned off.

CHAPTER FIVE

Benny and Becca walked arm in arm down the street, taking in the sights of the local shops and vendors. Market Place had a reputation for breeding two kinds of shops: the steadfast, famous stores with well-known names, and the cursed shops that frequently featured business for less than six months. Try as they might, most shop owners simply couldn't keep up with the times, and they often shut down overnight and quite unexpectedly. Benny liked to imagine that the spirits of previous owners haunted some of the shops, wandering their aisles and storefronts and searching for lost or forgotten stashes of money.

Becca walked along, asking him about his job and who his best clients were. He wasn't accustomed to this kind of conversation, mostly because women didn't often find his job interesting. Most women were impressed by his income but not by the details of his occupation. He had become familiar with a set list of easier, simpler words he could use to describe what he did. He wished that he could meet people who appreciated his work, but then again, he didn't care much for his job anyway. And yet, here he was, enjoying telling Becca about his job. Hell, he even laughed with her when he told some of his stories.

What was it about her that made things seem better? He'd told these stories many times before, but they felt fresh with her. She seemed to actually care about him and the things he'd done.

As they walked, he would point out buildings he'd had meetings in, or places where he'd had large lunch engagements. She burst with laughter when he told the story about having lunch with the mayor and how the mayor had thrown up right after the meal. "I take it we shouldn't get a meal there any time soon," she chuckled. "Nah, I'm sure it's fine now. Maybe just a snafu at the time," he laughed. "On second thought, maybe just stay away from the bisque."

The two made their way across the streets and alleys toward the park. They weren't really walking in any particular direction, and they had no intention of going to the park. The park just seemed like the best place to walk and talk. After the laughter died down from a particularly embarrassing story, he wiped a tear away and asked, "So, Becca, where do you work?" She laughed and looked away for a moment before replying, "Oh I work from home. I sell things online." "Ah, I see, a private business owner," he teased. "Such a glamorous life." "Hey, shut up, Big Bucks," she quipped, nudging him. "It pays the bills."

Benny laughed and rubbed his side, "Hey, take it easy. So, what do you sell? Do you have a product?" "No, not like that," she replied. "I sell things online for other people. I check sites where people are looking to sell something, and I sell it for them. I get the item, make a better looking sales page than they can, and I sell the item for more than they think they can get." "Ah," he said, rubbing his chin, "you're more of a dealer. That seems like an interesting business. I'd imagine there's money to be made doing that." She laughed and crossed her arms, "I do pretty well for myself. The trick is to make yourself seem more valuable than you really are, but it also helps to put yourself in the right place at the right time." He smiled and said, "I'm sure you have no trouble seeming valuable to people." She blushed and turned away from him.

Benny realized he was flirting with her. Here he was, flirting with a woman he barely knew, and he was a taken man. How could he do this to Karen? She had never been unfaithful to him. Well, he assumed she hadn't. They didn't really talk about that kind of thing. In a way, Karen had her own life and he had his. They were certainly a couple, but there was something missing. Rather, there had been something missing lately. He could see that, but he couldn't figure out what was missing from their relationship.

As if she sensed what he was thinking, Becca asked, "So, you make all that good money, but do you have anyone to share it with?" He coughed, "Oh, uh, yes. I have a girlfriend named Karen." "Ah," she said, almost with a sigh, "I bet she's a classy uptown lady." He chuckled, "Yeah, she's pretty great. She likes to think of herself as an uptown lady, but I think she truly..." He was cut short by the ringing of his cellphone. He realized he hadn't been checking the time and pulled the ringing phone from his pocket. The time read "7:30 P.M." Karen was calling, just as she always did after dinner. "It's her. Let me take this, and I'll be right back," he said, stepping away from Becca.

He answered the call and turned his attention away from Becca. "Hey honey. How was dinner? Good, glad to... Oh wow, that must... yeah, that must have been expensive. Was the... not that great? That's a shame. You'd think they'd make better... right. Well at least you didn't... oh you had to buy your own drinks. Well that does... well I mean they can't... right, but if everyone gets a drink... yeah, I guess you're right. It's not... yeah, they should cover the tab too. So are you... okay, well, have fun with the girls. Me? Oh I'm still out. Just walking... no, I have my coat. I should be... I won't stay out late. Don't worry. I met someone while walking." At this, he turned to Becca and looked at her. She was staring back up the street at something. "He was out walking in the park. Nice guy, owns his own business. Yeah... he's... oh you have to go? Okay, be safe tonight... will do. I love you too. Bye." Benny closed the phone.

He had just lied. He had lied to Karen. *I had to do that, I couldn't tell her I'm with another woman. She'd freak out and assume the worst*, he argued with his conscience. He felt guilty, though. He'd never lied to Karen before. He made it a point to always be honest with her, and he prided himself on his honesty. But then, he thought about how many times tonight he hadn't been honest. He hadn't told her about wanting to kill himself. He hadn't told her about how miserable he was. And he hadn't told her about Becca, not that there was anything to tell.

Benny returned from his thoughts and rejoined Becca. "Sorry about that. She wanted to talk for a while." She laughed, "I know, I heard. Please, tell me more about this guy you met. I'm sure he was a really great guy." This time, it was Benny's turn to grow red with embarrassment. "Oh, you heard that," He sighed. "Yep, and I must say, I had hoped that I don't look very manly. Maybe I need to run more," she joked, rubbing her stomach and ribs. He sighed and rubbed the back of his head. "I'm sorry. She can be very jealous, and I didn't want her freaking out." "It's okay," she said with a grin, stepping closer to him. "I like the scandal of it." Taking his arm again, they walked under the archway and further into the park.

There it is again, he thought. *I feel that rush. Am I enjoying this? I'm basically courting another woman, and she knows it. This girl is trouble, but the real problem is that I think I like it.* He considered how often Karen made him feel this way, or how often he felt the rush with her. There was really nothing wrong with Karen. She was a good woman who loved him and appreciated him. She took care of him when he needed her, and she was always there for him. It was then that Benny began to ask himself if that were really true. Did Karen give him everything he needed? Did Karen really appreciate him?

The thought nagged at Benny. He was going to kill himself, or at least try. He fully intended to do so, and it didn't make much sense to do so if he felt supported by Karen. Did this happen overnight, or had he felt this neglect for a while? He tried to think, but he couldn't really recall a time or particular event where this started. Things just seemed different lately. Was it Karen, or was it something in him? He really didn't know.

Sensing they hadn't spoken in a while, Benny broke his awkward silence, and the two talked of their personal pasts. They mostly talked in generalities, neither digging too deep into personal areas. He couldn't help but notice how natural conversation seemed with Becca. That might have been due to there being no danger in disappointing her or causing her unease. *If she dislikes me, she'll just go away and things will resume as they were*, he considered. *She doesn't have to be a part of my life, what little is left of it.* And yet, he found himself hating the idea of her leaving.

As they walked, he couldn't help but tell stories of the park and his firm's involvement with the development. He even told of some personal experiences, many of which ended in embarrassment for him. She always seemed interested in his stories, though he couldn't really tell if she were faking it. Benny simply enjoyed talking to her and being heard. The feeling was fresh to him, something he didn't often experience. His job never afforded him time for conversation with anyone, and Karen wasn't so hot at listening. A light flickered behind Benny's eyes, and he said, "Come on. I want to show you something."

Leading her past the fences and the small amphitheater, he drew her to a patch of trees that lined the side of the grounds. "Duck your head. It's just over here," he advised, bending and holding his hand out to her. They tucked under the tree line and back to an oak tree by a short shrub. The mulch still had the signs of disturbance from hours before. A squirrel darted from the bush and dashed across a nearby trunk and branch. "This is my spot," he said, gesturing as if it were a treasure or a rare sight. "I come here when I need to be alone, or when I need to think. I found it one day while throwing a Frisbee with my cousin from Georgia." She smiled and walked to the tree. Dusting off the mulch, she crouched down and sat next to the base. She looked up at him and patted the mulch next to her. Trying to not grin like an idiot, he joined her next to the tree.

From their seat, they could see through the break in the tree and towards the city skyline. In the fall, businesses and skyscrapers put up lights adorning the tops and sides of the businesses, and even office workers decorated their desks with lights. The whole thing made for a beautiful sight, and Benny considered this spot to be the best view in the city. He had spent many nights down there, looking up at the lights, but he had never spent that time with anyone. Sure, he'd shown the spot to Karen and even to his cousin or a friend that happened to visit. But he'd never shared the lights. That was something he reserved for himself. In a way, knowing that this existed made him feel significant, like he was the keeper of a great treasure. Things like that were the only moments that made Benny feel like he mattered.

"This is a pretty great spot. You get to see a lot of wonderful things," she said, scooting a little closer to him. "Yeah, the lights weren't on when I first found this place. I only saw them by chance one night when I came here. I make it a tradition to come here at least once a month and see the lights, though that's really best spent during the fall and winter months," he replied, taking full notice of her moving closer to him. The two sat for several minutes in silence, staring up at the lights. Somewhere in that time, and Benny couldn't be certain that she meant to, Becca put her head on his shoulder. She was resting her head about half on his shoulder and half against the tree, but he decided that he would believe it was one hundred percent on his shoulder. It was in that moment that Benny noticed he felt happy. He felt like he was connecting with someone on a level he hadn't connected before. This felt natural, and he found himself treasuring this moment.

"Thank you for bringing me here," she sighed. "I needed this tonight. I've been so stressed out with work, and I just needed a chance to unwind and relax." "My pleasure," Benny replied, smiling wide enough that he was sure she could feel his facial expression. "I'm glad someone else can appreciate this place, especially when you're stressed out." She chuckled, "I really shouldn't be. My job is easy, and I shouldn't get so worked up about it. Maybe that's not what upsets me. Maybe it's just the nature of my job. Maybe it's my life right now." Benny turned his head towards her, looking down but barely moving so as not to disturb her. "What do you mean? Don't you like selling things for people? That seems like a fun, entertaining business." She paused, taking a long breath: "It is, and it isn't. It's not the kind of job you want forever. I don't really want it any more, to be honest. Lately, I feel lost. I feel like I'm not doing anything with my life." She sat up, pulling her legs up to herself and wrapping her arms around them. "I didn't think I'd be doing this still, and I just, I don't know, I thought I'd be someone else. I just thought life would go a different way, and I know that I'm only twenty-seven, but I thought I'd be on my way to my future by now, whatever the hell it's supposed to be."

Benny sat up, and turned completely towards her. "I know exactly what you mean," Benny said, putting a hand to her shoulder. "I hate my life. I hate my job, I hate my apartment, and I hate this city. I treasure places like this because they make me forget how miserable I am. And that's the problem, because I have a fantastic job and a great apartment. I have a relationship that makes me happy, at least most of the time. All of those things should offer confirmation that I'm fine, that I have plenty of purpose. But lately, I feel lost. I feel like I don't belong, like I don't matter." He took a deep breath, feeling the cool air of the evening enter his warm lungs. "You know," he finally said after a pause, "I feel alone. I know that's silly, but I just feel alone. I can be around a crowd all day, surrounded by people I know, and yet I still feel so lonely and out of place. Sometimes, I feel more alone when I'm with people than when I'm here by myself." Looking into her eyes, he could see she understood him. She felt what he felt, and she knew the thoughts he had been thinking for what seemed like years now. Perhaps they were alike in more ways than he could ever have expected.

"I have to tell someone something, and I think it should be you," he said, lowering his voice a little. Benny felt the hairs on his arm prickling. He knew he was about to share more with her than he'd shared with anyone. "Tonight, here in this spot, I was going to kill myself." Becca didn't say a word. Her eyes widened ever so slightly, and her mouth broke open gently.

"Here?"

"Yes, Becca. I'm so miserable. I didn't want to live another minute, and I planned on killing myself. I chose to do it here, under my favorite tree."

"Is that why you brought me here?"

"No, I never intended to tell you any of this. I couldn't do it. When the time came, I just couldn't do it."

"Why? Why would you kill yourself?"

Benny paused, looking for an answer.

"I don't know. I wanted to, but mostly because it seemed like the answer to my problems, to my questions. I just don't have any of the answers that I wanted to have in my life by now. I wanted to know so much more than I do. And I wanted to be happy. I just don't think a person on Earth would really care if I wasn't here anymore."

He reached into his pocket and drew out the pistol. He held it timidly, looking down at it and thinking over the words he had just said. It was then that words began to come to his mouth, as if they'd made their way through his body and brain without anyone checking to see if they were good words. Before he could stop himself, he said, "But then I met you, and now I'm not so sure I want to end it all." He tried to hide the fact that he was completely embarrassed to say that. He felt like screaming, like every emotion in his body was rushing up out of his throat, begging to break the silence.

Becca put a hand to his face. His face rose to meet hers. She looked as if she might cry. Then, her eyes darted a little, and she seemed to think of something. Pulling her hand from his face, she took a short, quick breath. "I shouldn't have done this. I shouldn't be here," she said, looking about herself. Benny quickly pocketed the gun and put a hand on hers, trying to calm her. "No, it's okay," he quickly stammered. "I'm not going to kill myself. I don't think so. I just... it's okay. I won't. Just calm down." But she was already getting to her feet, She was breathing heavier now, looking at him with a kind of longing concern. "I need to get away from you. You don't need to be around me. I'll only hurt you and make this worse." She started for the tree line. He reached out to her: "Wait, I promise. I won't do this. I didn't mean to scare you. Just come back." Becca stopped, looking back at Benny. She opened her mouth to say something, but no words came. She smiled, her eyes locked with his, and darted through the trees.

Benny watched her cross the grass. As she moved, she looked to her left and stopped. She seemed to be staring at something by the road nearby. Then, she walked, shoving her hands into the pockets of her fleece. He watched her disappear past the fountains and up the steps. Slumping back against the tree, his heart sank. He blew it. He had ruined the one seemingly good thing going for him. How could he be so stupid as to scare her off like that? She probably thought he was a weird loser. Suddenly, the thought of suicide seemed like a great idea. "Why not just shoot myself?" Benny said quietly to himself. "Who cares? I don't matter."

Benny pulled the gun from his pocket and stared at it. Maybe the gun had the answers he needed. Maybe he just wasn't fit for this world. He'd tried so many times to get it all right, but nothing he did lasted. He felt worthless. A rage began brewing in his stomach, and, growling with rage, he let out a groan and threw the gun as hard as he could into the mulch. The gun barrel jammed down into the dirt. Benny picked the gun up and threw it down again. He sat there, breathing heavy and gritting his teeth. The best thing that had happened to him in a long while just walked away, and all because he was an idiot. Benny was hopeless, and he knew it. "I should do it, put an end to this. There's no reason not to," he said in a hushed, angry voice. He thought about it, but something nagged at him. It was something Becca said to him.

She had said that she would hurt him. He pondered that, considering what her words meant. How could she hurt him, when he was thinking of shooting himself? She couldn't do anything to him that he couldn't already and wouldn't already do to himself. So why did she seem scared for him? He couldn't get the thought out of his head. Was she in trouble? Or was he?

Picking up the gun, he dusted the mulch and dirt off the

body. He stood, pocketing the pistol and ducking out of the break in the tree line. As he exited his hidden grove, he looked around, hoping he'd see her standing somewhere, but she was gone. He had no idea where she lived or where she was going, and he had no promise of seeing her again. Benny considered that he could simply wait in the frozen yogurt shop until she came back, but they'd never stay open long enough, and that bordered on stalker material. He resigned to his fate of never seeing her again and started walking through the park, even though he had no destination in mind.

As he crossed the park, he found himself lost in a world of thought. His anger at upsetting her felt less like a consuming fire and more like the opening to a well of which he couldn't climb out. If he wasn't depressed before, he certainly was now. Things seemed bleak for his evening, and he just didn't see a way to brighten his spirits. He wished he could just see her once more and tell her things were okay and she didn't have to go. As he walked, his attention stayed on his thoughts, never drifting to anything around him. His attention especially didn't fall on the dark grey van, slowly pulling from the parallel space next to the tree line and creeping along a few yards behind him. He didn't notice the two men in the front seats, staring at him, and he certainly didn't notice that the headlights were still turned off.

CHAPTER SIX

As he wandered through the park, Benny started to feel angry. He was angry, but not because he had upset Becca. No, Benny was angry because he had been close to having something new. For one brief moment, he had a reason to live. He had a reason to keep going, to look forward to that something new. In fact, he had, though briefly, actually thought himself stupid for even thinking of killing himself.

With no idea of what to do next, or even where he wanted to go next, Benny simply walked. He wandered through the park, up the steps and back to the city square. As he walked, a dark grey van shadowed his path, creeping slowly behind him, maintaining at least a few yards of distance. The driver watched him like a wolf eyeing a wounded prey. The passenger spoke on a cellphone, maintaining a calm composure and keeping his eyes on Benny.

Benny saw none of this, as he kept his head buried in the street. Where should he go? What could he do? Could he find her, or was that a fruitless waste of effort? Maybe the best thing to do would be to give up. Benny wasn't sure, but he needed something. If he didn't feel lost before, he certainly did now.

Maybe what he needed was to see the lights of the square. The night life of Market Place would be hitting its apex right about now, and the fall lights would be glowing, shining good feelings down on the shoppers and guests. Perhaps that would clear his head, or at least give him some kind of relief. To be taken so abruptly from that great moment beneath the tree, Benny felt like a child that had received a new toy only to have it broken moments later. He wanted that moment back. He would have given anything to be back with her.

As he crossed the concrete bridge, he kept his gaze on the walk. He did not look down to see the van merge violently across three lanes, attempting to catch his movements. Cutting off a large pick up, the van swerved around the corner, sneaking quickly into a parallel space beside the walk. From there, the passenger could see Benny walking the concrete bridge across the boulevard. He watched as Benny descended the short flight of stairs at the end of the walk, swung his foot to kick a soda can on the sidewalk, missed, and almost fell into a flower box. The driver and passenger exchanged a glance, making little to no changes in facial expression except for a small grin grazing their lips.

Benny regained his composure. A day or two before, he would have looked to see if anyone saw him stumble like that, but not today. Today, he didn't care. He didn't care what anyone thought or wanted of him. He rather wished that this had been the time that he and Kyle had run into each other. He would have unloaded his grief and anger on Kyle. Kyle didn't deserve that, but Benny didn't care. He wanted to yell at someone. He wanted to scream, to run into the street. He wanted to be hit by a car.

Behind him, a van screeched to a stop. Benny turned, startled by the sound of his dream coming to life, but it was just a dark gray van stopping suddenly as a child crossed the street with her parents. The driver waved them on, looking rather surly over his drive being interrupted. The passenger studied a cellphone, looked up at Benny, looked away with a brief word, and then returned his attention to his cell phone. The two of them sat for a moment longer before turning left up a one-way street. Benny marveled at how rude they could be and how dangerous they were, but he knew plenty of bad drivers in this city. People in town drove with barely any regard for the safety of others, and he'd become accustomed to the attitude.

Resuming his sulking, he trudged on, wandering the square. Maybe he was hungry? No, that wasn't it. Maybe he was cold and needed to warm up? No, that wasn't the problem either. "I'm glad I'm cold, it matches the feeling in my cold, broken heart," he mumbled to himself. He promptly grimaced at how disgustingly pathetic that statement had been. *You should go home and write poetry all night,* he moaned, mocking himself for being so dramatic. *She was just one woman. Who cares about her? She clearly doesn't care about you. If she did, she wouldn't have run off like that.* Benny wanted to lock her out of his mind, but nothing seemed to help.

As he entered the square of Market Place, he looked about himself at the lights and decorations. He marveled at how soon they were putting up holiday decorations, but then again, that seemed to be the mentality of everyone running a business lately. He'd even been working with the firm's accounts for several months prior, arranging Thanksgiving and Christmas events. He couldn't believe he was coordinating Christmas engagements in late September. Maybe that was why he hated his job. The tasks took the joy out of the holidays. He dreaded the Christmas season, because he knew that it brought nothing but long hours and public events.

At the far northern end of Market Place, the dark grey van rolled into a diagonal space. With the headlights still off, the faces of the driver and passenger could barely be seen, apart from the overhead street lamps and the light of the passenger's glowing cell phone screen. The two sat, watching Benny as he wandered through the square. They watched as he stopped at a few shop windows, peering in at the displays and shoppers. The passenger silenced his phone three times, grinning a little bigger each time it rang. On the fourth call, he even let out a short chuckle. The phone promptly went silent, as if intimidated by his laugh.

Benny simply didn't know what to do. He didn't know if he wanted to live or die. No, that was a lie. Benny knew. He'd known since she ran. He wanted to die. He wanted to give up. He was so angry that he couldn't think of anything else. He just needed a place to end it all. The park could have been that place, but he didn't want to run the risk of Becca coming back to find him. He couldn't hurt her, even though he barely knew her. She was something special, and he just couldn't do that to her.

Considering the evening's events, he knew that the best course of action was to return home. He needed to end his life in his apartment. That was the only place that made sense. He should have done it there when he had the chance. Had he done it there, he could have avoided meeting her. He didn't love her, but he certainly felt something for her. "Who ever said 'It is better to have loved and lost than to never have loved at all' can go to hell," Benny grumbled out loud, somehow comforted by the idea of announcing this to the world. And so, setting his sights on his apartment, he marched toward his inevitable end.

As they watched him stride out of the square, the two men started the van and pulled out from their space. They turned down Main and followed him to the corner of Wershuck Avenue and Main Street. He was moving much faster now, almost power-walking. The driver maintained an invisible distance while the passenger kept an eye on him. Benny marched on unaware of his motorized stalkers lurking behind. He looked up and could see the light of his apartment. He had left a lamp on. Normally, he would have immediately worried about the cost of electricity and how his bill might be higher for this, but he didn't worry tonight. Not anymore, at least. Benny was done. He didn't even wait for the crossing sign to change as he crossed the street to his apartment.

The van eased to a stop at the corner, watching him move towards the stoop of the old Kernley Building. The street was quiet and empty, almost to the point of abandoned. The two men looked at each other and nodded, as if they knew the drill from here. As he walked the few remaining feet to the stoop, the driver pulled the van into the parallel spaces of the street side parking. He stopped about twenty feet from the stoop and watched Benny turn to the steps.

Benny had reached his stoop. A couple of concrete steps

more and he would be in his apartment. He had accepted his fate and made peace with the choices that led him here. Stopping at the top of the stoop, he paused and turned his head back toward the city. He thought of her once more, wondering where she was and what she was doing at this very minute. Odds are, she wasn't thinking of him, and he knew that perfectly well. A sigh broke the silence of his gaze, and he turned to the door leading into the complex. It was at this moment that his phone rang.

He turned, sighing and reaching into his pocket. He didn't have to look to know who was calling. *It must be close to 8:30,* he thought, acknowledging that the time had come for another chat. Sure enough, Karen's name was once again burning across his phone. He walked back down the stoop and sat on the front steps. He hovered his thumb over the answer button, ready to lie to his girlfriend about how happy he was. This time, however, something inside him snapped. Benny thought about her, and he thought about how she would never understand what he was going through. She would probably laugh at him and never even begin to fathom what kind of pressure he could be under, what kind of expectations he had to meet every day. So, for the first time in a very, very long time, he willingly didn't answer the phone. He watched the call ring over and over again until the phone finally stopped chiming. Pocketing the phone once more, he stood and turned to go up the steps.

In less time than he could gather his senses to comprehend, a large man's fists clenched together struck Benny from behind. He was down on his knees, being gagged by a handkerchief that smelled a bit like copper. The man threw a black sack over his head and tossed him into the side of an open van. Benny was surrounded by black as he slid onto the van's cold metal floor and slammed his head into the side of the panel. He screamed, but not a soul could hear him through the gag. Benny fumbled in the dark, but realized that a large zip tie bound his hands together. He was alone, trapped in the back of this now quickly moving and abusively turbulent van. As the panic set further in, Benny's last rational thought, before his panicked screaming fit, was of the phone. He realized that, if he had answered the phone, Karen would have heard his attacker. She could have called the police. Instead, he had let the call go to Voicemail.

He spent the next ten to fifteen minutes kicking, screaming, crying, rolling, and even jumping at times, trying to break free of the zip tie on his wrists or do something to further his escape. Without really knowing how, he managed to get his hands down over his legs and in front of him. At least with this advantage, he could grab things or fight back a little against his attackers. Considering the size of the man that grabbed him though, Benny imagined he'd probably have to work pretty hard. After finally calming down and coming to a clearer head, he tried to think of the next thing to do. He tried pulling the sack off of his head, but that too was tied onto him. He tried finding door handles inside the van, but they had all been removed. Scooting closer to the dividing wall of the van's front, he tried listening for conversation, but he couldn't make out a single word.

Benny was trapped, alone and scared. He had no idea what these men wanted, but he was sure it wouldn't end well. They'd probably shoot him once they were done with whatever they planned to do with him. He suddenly sat up stiffly, remembering the pistol in his pocket. Had they taken it? Did they know he had one? He tried to reach his pocket, but struggling against his restraints proved to be challenging. Finally, after contorting himself in a highly awkward manner, he finally reached his pocket. He padded the fabric to feel the shape of the pistol, but it was not there. They took the gun. He knew it now. The big guy must have felt it in his pocket and taken it before he threw Benny in the van.

His heart sank. That gun had been his chance to break free. He sat against the walls of the van, feeling the despair set in. And then he noticed the metal scraping. It was the sound of something, somewhat small and metal, scooting across the floor of the van. It took several moments for Benny to realize the sound he was hearing was the sound of the gun sliding around the empty van bed. Scrambling to his knees, Benny tried to listen for the gun's echoes, as he could not see through the hood. A scrape here, a scrape there, but none of the sounds gave him any indication of location. He slowly crept across the van floor, pawing and scooping, hoping the gun would fall into his hands. After several panicked moments of searching, he ceased his blind groping, convinced that hope was lost.

Guiding himself back to his corner, Benny collapsed into his previous seat only to bark in pain. He had sat down on something quite hard, something that he had missed previously. Thrusting his hand down to the floor, he felt the cool, slightly rough metal of the .22 caliber pistol he was previously carrying. He felt a massive rush of adrenaline, knowing there might be hope. He could fight back, and he might escape. He could certainly shoot his captors, assuming he could hit them with a few shots without seeing a thing. He had no idea how he would ever get the hood off, but he assume he'd figure that out after escaping.

The van slowed, and Benny felt the engine idling. They had stopped. Benny readied himself for anything. They could reach in and throw him out. He could be left alone and helpless wherever they were. He heard soft footsteps outside. The two men were walking away from the van. He began to panic. Were they abandoning him? He would surely starve. This couldn't be the end. He tried to calm himself, but the uncertainty of his predicament kept his heart racing. Moments later, the sound of footsteps returned. The two men were walking at a brisk pace, and, judging from the faint sounds of muffled screaming, he assumed they were bringing someone. That must have been the nature of this stop, to pick up another victim.

Benny steadied himself against the wall of the van. Should he draw his pistol? He would only be able to make out the faintest light changes, and he certainly wouldn't see anyone. He decided to pocket the pistol and wait for the right time to strike. The doors of the van flew open, and the two men shoved the body of their new victim into the van. He wanted to know who it was, but considering the unknown guest was moaning in the same way he had, he could assume this person was gagged as well. *Of course, there's also the chance that this person is dangerous,* he thought. *This person may not be too happy to be back here. What if I get hurt?* His best bet lay in sitting still and minding his own business.

He couldn't say for certain how long they had been driving, but it couldn't have been longer than fifteen to twenty minutes. Towards the end of the drive, the van had pulled into a graveled area. Slowly coming to a stop, Benny felt the van rock gently and assumed they had reached their destination. He heard the footsteps moving around the van. This was it. He knew they were coming now. He tried to calm himself as the doors cracked open. The men stepped into the van. They seemed to be moving toward Benny. He couldn't understand why they would take him first, but he let them grab him and lift him up. Struggling seemed pointless.

Lifting him by his bound arms, one of the men pulled him to his feet and led him forward. The bag on his head still blocked out all light, providing him no sense of where they had stopped. He tried to calm his breathing, thinking that he might be able to hear something that would indicate where they had taken him. The man leading him stepped down and pulled Benny out of the van. "Sit," the strong voice instructed. Benny sat at the lip of the van's bed.

Benny was just beginning to formulate an awkward plan involving crying and maybe asking to pee somewhere so that he could "make a break for it" when he heard one of the men leading the other victim. The victim was barking at the man, but Benny couldn't make out a single word. *They must have gagged him as well.* As the victim reached the edge of the van's bed, the mouth gag must have begun to slip loose, because the victim had gained the ability to speak. Benny was surprised to hear the voice of a woman yelling at the two men: "You idiots are going to regret this. I've told you a hundred times that I'm not interested in this. You two can go to hell for all I care. You do not want to cross me, because I am a loose damn cannon right now." She sat with a thud. Benny heard the men snip the zip tie off of her hood and pull the hood from her head. She groaned and continued her tirade. "You will regret every minute of this stupid charade. There's nothing you can do to me that'll make me change my mind."

Benny felt the hands of one of the men around his neck. The zip tie fell loose. The man pulled the hood quickly from his face. Squinting at the flash of bright lights, he began to focus on the faces of two gruff looking men, one shorter and one taller. He turned his confused eyes to his fellow captive. He almost burst with a scream at the sight of Becca. He tried to say something, but all that really came out was a small bark/squeal. Becca turned her head, looked into Benny's wide eyes, hung her head, and sighed. "Son of a bitch."

CHAPTER SEVEN

The day couldn't possibly be a better one for jogging. The sun, hiding half behind the soft gray clouds of the afternoon sky, gave just enough light to keep the streets from being chilly. Becca stopped at a crosswalk and adjusted her fleece and tank top. For some reason, this particular fleece always rode up on her when she jogged, dragging the tank top with it. She assumed it was her fault for buying the fleece a size too large, but, considering she'd lost five pounds already, she couldn't have planned for the fleece's poor fit.

Becca detested tight, stretchy clothing. She didn't mind her tank top hugging her curves, because the tank top was soft and gave when she twisted or bent. She had even begun to love seeing her curves in the mirror, a definite gain in her quest to lose weight. This fleece, however, always got in the way. The fabric often gathered under her arms and twisted around her stomach. She should have gotten rid of the thing and purchased a new, slimmer one, but she liked remembering where she had come from in her weight loss.

Over the past month, she had worked hard to better herself. Her weight loss was going swimmingly, and she had started working on getting a legitimate career going. Best of all, she barely heard from her ex lately. He hadn't called in two weeks, and she had all but forgotten the feeling of missing him. She wished that she could let go of the guilt and anguish from her past, but she knew that this would come with time. Time was certainly something of which she had plenty, and she relished in this thought.

As she stood at the crosswalk, she debated her path. She could jog up the street to the right and pass the old museum. She loved to see the marble arches and the heavy brass doors, and she often stopped in the lobby to simply rest and enjoy the atmosphere. Sometimes, the security would ask her to leave, but that only really happened when the one guy was there, and he was a fat loser anyway.

Maybe I could just call it quits for today, she thought, contemplating a break in the open field area. It had been a while since she had stopped to lie down in the grass, and considering it was the middle of the month, the landscaping crew probably hadn't cut the grass yet. That meant the blades of grass would be tall and soft, and they might even still be warm from the sun. Granted, they wouldn't be "summer grass warm," but she would take what she could get.

She checked her watch: 4:28 PM. She should really start thinking about dinner soon. Becca tried to eat healthy. She always considered the calories of her meals or snacks during the day, but her problem lay in the fact that she often considered those calories hours after eating. She had heard that the best practice for proper exercise dining was to never eat less than an hour before a workout or to eat roughly thirty minutes after exercise. Since her apartment was usually the destination after her exercise, she never had trouble eating on time, but she still struggled with making something healthy.. Though she'd tried for at least a year, she still hadn't picked up the concept that frozen pizza isn't a proper post-workout food and stimulant.

Still, despite her poor diet ("Is it really fair to call it a poor diet? I think 'awesome diet' better describes it," she often said), she took otherwise fine care of herself. And, as of late, that hard work was beginning to really show. She often caught herself noticing her figure in the mirror. So what if she liked the way her body looked now? She had every right to enjoy. Becca came from a long line of Eastern European women, and she had always been full figured. Early in her weight loss, she had taught herself that full-figured did not mean the same thing as overweight, and so she took pride in maintaining her new curvy figure.

Maybe it was the air, maybe it was the time of year, or maybe it was some other devil of a drive, but, more and more, Becca found herself wanting to be wanted. Sure, her ex gave her plenty of attention, but it was all unwanted. The guy was a creep and an equally poor human being. No, she wanted to be desired by someone who respected her. She wanted someone to look at her as more than just "a hot ass and a nice rack." She despised him for that. He loved to joke that he had acquired the hottest body in the business. The first time, the line was kind of charming, but after countless uses and especially in public, the joke got old fast. She wanted someone new, someone who saw into the real her.

Thinking about her past brought back so much anxiety, so she decided to keep running. Having left the park, she thought about where to visit next in her spontaneous tour of the city. The best route would be over the sky-walk that crossed the boulevard. She loved to see the cars, and the trail led her right into Market Place. If nothing else, she'd at least get some great sights in before heading home. She checked the crossing sign, looked both ways, and crossed the street to the stair set leading to the skywalk.

The wind whipped across the concrete walkway. She loved that sound. It always sounded like a dramatic sound effect from a movie, especially the kind that would indicate a change was coming. Just like that, her blues were gone. She felt much better, and she felt herself jogging happily away from her past.

As she neared the steps, she slowed her pace to make sure the steps weren't slick. The steps of the walkway had been resurfaced, but, for some reason, the steps were extra slick after it had rained. *I hope no one is watching, because if I fall, I'm going to feel really stupid.* As if having been called there by duty, she caught the eyes of someone: a very, very cute guy. *Oh great, an audience,* she thought, grinning to herself. *Wait... is he staring? Oh. Oh yes he is.*

That's right, girl. A cute guy is staring at you.

Becca felt her blood rush. This guy was actually staring at her. Hell, he was flat out drooling. She slowed down a little more, making sure he got a nice long look. Normally, if a guy stared at her for an extended length of time, that creeped her out, whether he was cute or not. This guy, however, was different. He wasn't undressing her with his eyes. He was staring at her as a whole. She could see it in his face. This was different, and she loved it. *Man, I'm a mess right now, and he's still staring,* she chuckled to herself.

Catching a glimpse of the crossing signal, she decided to keep going and not stop. She'd probably just ruin the moment by saying something stupid. She decided to keep this moment as a reminder of why she was working so hard on herself. Hopping up onto the sidewalk, she took a left and headed for Market Place.

She was feeling good. She'd just come down from the rush of being admired by an attractive man, which she was still chuckling about. *I've been jogging for an hour. There's no way I look my best right now. I'm probably not even 'presentable,' whatever the hell that means.* Keeping herself motivated hadn't really been a challenge, but she still liked reaffirmation that her hard work was paying off. Moments like the one back at the foot of the sky-walk certainly did that.

Feeling a bit more energetic, she decided to keep running for another thirty minutes. She made several laps around Market Place before turning her attention to heading home to her apartment. Her stomach had begun to roar, and she thought it best to tame the wild beast with some dinner. Turning left outside Market Place, she made a right at the next light and walked down Macon Street toward her apartment.

As she passed the small convenience store on her right, she noticed they had a sale on their canned foods. It was then that she remembered her trip to the grocer that she had neglected to take. She had no food at home, at least none worth eating. *Looks like I'm dining out tonight,* she thought while grinning, enjoying the chance to live a little. She'd never been very good with money, and she tried her best to save as much as she could, but she still liked any and all chances to live a little frivolously.

Making an abrupt U-turn, she headed back to Market Place. She began thinking of the different restaurants, trying to decide what she felt like tonight. She was doing a terrible job of not choosing places that were unhealthy and counterproductive for her. *Surely there's somewhere in Market Place I can go that won't ruin the effort I've made so far,* she whined, wracking her brain to think of somewhere. Market Place was inviting and pleasant, but the shop owners and restaurateurs hadn't done a very good job creating variety in the area. Sure, there were plenty of places to eat, but nothing really wild. Apart from the Greek restaurant and the sushi house, there really weren't many places to shake up the daily routine of diners.

The crowd in Market Place wasn't particularly heavy at this time, which would mean she could find a good seat just about anywhere. The question still remained as to where she would eat, and her stomach grew more and more impatient by the minute. She finally settled on the new sandwich shop on the corner. The place had been there less than six months, and the owner still refused to do any kind of advertising or even put up signs in the area. The name of the place was extremely vague, like an inside joke shared between someone with no friends. The whole thing had actually been pretty big news when the restaurant opened, and the owner had made it clear through several interviews that she did not believe in advertising and promoting. At one point, she had even said, "Trust me, the food will speak for itself." She was right in a way. Customers used the same words to describe the food as the place itself: "Eh," "it's okay," and "I like it, I guess." No one really went there unless they wanted something specific off the menu.

Becca liked their heroes, as they always put extra meat on them. She also liked the fact that they used too much spice, something she'd never seen anyone do to a sandwich. To her, the place was a weird, quirky hodgepodge of ideas and plans for a sandwich shop, none of which came together in any functional or logical way. She liked that though. The shop just felt like a weird apartment out of which someone decided to sell sandwiches, and she strangely felt at home there.

After ordering her meal, she took her drink cup to the soda fountain and filled it with water. This was a practice she always insisted on doing, despite the fact that they sold bottled water. To her, she needed to stand in front of the soda fountain and tell herself, "You can't have any of these." That made her feel strong and powerful, rather than being a slave to sugary sodas. She was proud of this trait, and she smiled over her hard work. She would never admit that she might actually burn the building down just to have a cup of Mountain Dew.

Sitting down to her favorite booth, she relaxed, feeling her calves and thighs release the tension. She hadn't taken a break since she started jogging, and she could feel the burn. Becca liked feeling that burn. She often thought that, if it weren't for the immediate sensation of lactic acid building up in her muscles and then washing away, she would never enjoy exercise. Her jogs were something she looked forward to every day, and she hated missing them. She rarely skipped, unless she'd had a long job or felt ill. Sometimes, she said she felt ill, but the truth was she was really enjoying a terrible movie on TV. Bad movies were her guilty pleasure.

Her smartphone began ringing. She unzipped the pocket of her running pants and pulled the phone out. The number was one she did not recognize, and her practice was to never answer an unregistered number. She rarely received calls or texts from unregistered numbers, so she never, ever answered them. She despised being bothered, especially on her cell phone. To her, getting a call from a number she didn't recognize was the same as having a stranger just walk into her home. Silencing the call, she sat the phone down next to her.

Her food arrived (the sandwich shop prided itself on bringing the food to the table, a service she wasn't certain merited a tip), and she checked it for proper ingredients. The shop was notorious for not catching requests like "no mayo" or "hold the tomato." They didn't seem negligent, but they also didn't seem like they were terribly concerned about customer backlash. Her sandwich having passed the standard of approval, she set to the task of devouring. She had barely finished her first bite when her phone rang again.

She picked it up to find the same number calling this time. No Voicemail notification appeared in the top bar, indicating that the caller hadn't left one previously. *Who are you, and what exactly do you want?* This time, she denied the call, knowing that would send the call directly to voicemail. She had made sure, when she first bought her phone, to leave a very succinct message that spelled out exactly what she expected of every caller: "Hi, you've reached Becca. If you've got something to say, leave it. If not, that's cool too. Just buzz off." The message seemed clear to her. Someone behind this number wasn't taking the hint.

Setting her phone down, she picked up her sandwich to take a bite, but the phone rang again. "You again?" she groaned audibly. She denied the call and set her phone to vibrate. Perhaps now she would have some peace while she dined. She set the phone down, took a bite, and the phone rang again. She denied the call, took a bite, and the phone rang. Her entire meal consisted of this, her patience growing thinner with each call. *Who the hell thinks they can just keep calling me? Take a hint, you jerk. I don't want to talk to someone I don't know. Leave a message or buzz off,* she raged in her head, grinding her teeth in frustration.

Her meal complete, she stood and took her tray to the garbage. As she dumped the contents into the trash, she accidentally dropped her water cup into the trash as well. "Great, just great," she whined, pounding her fist gently into the garbage bin. She knew that the store didn't give new cups to customers. Apparently the restaurant couldn't handle the rising cost of drinkware. She returned to her booth and grabbed her phone. She had missed two calls from the same number while at the garbage can. "Sheesh, get a life," she muttered under her breath.

As she stepped out of the sandwich shop, her phone rang once more. She considered throwing the phone away, but she calmed herself. *The weirdo will just stop calling. Surely they'll give up. It's probably some stupid collections agency or something,* she scoffed, shrugging off the worry and concern. Except, she knew she didn't have any past due bills, and she'd never seen a business call more than twice. When her phone rang for what must have been the twelfth time in an hour, she started to worry. Who the hell would be calling her like this? Why would they keep calling when she always ignored the call or even sent it directly to Voicemail? Whoever was calling her wanted to talk very badly, and she was growing more and more concerned and impatient

The phone had stopped ringing. In total, she had received fifteen calls in the span of an hour. The person might have called more, but she couldn't be certain, as she had tried to put the whole thing out of her mind. By now, she was frustrated and irritable. In fifteen calls, not once had the caller left a Voicemail. "What a jerk," she hissed, frustrated enough to talk to herself. "Somebody needs to learn some respect and courtesy." She paced around the square, hoping that her foul mood would go away. Sadly, her angst seemed to fester with time. *Who the hell doesn't leave a stupid voice mail?* She gritted her teeth, trying her best to not become annoyed. *What kind of moronic psycho calls that much and refuses to leave a Voice mail at any time?*

Deciding that she deserved a treat for her hard work and dinner interruption, she decided to hit up her favorite desert parlor, Lee's Freeze. She'd been a fan of the shop since it opened, but she'd not been a frequent customer, at least not as much as she'd liked to have been. Frozen yogurt wasn't exactly the best friend to a person looking to lose weight, and her ex hadn't been a fan even before she was trying to lose weight. Now that she was single and working out, she tried to visit the place at least once every two weeks. Everyone working out should have a treat, and she felt that Lee's could be her treat.

Stepping up to the doors, she smiled, seeing the families gathered inside. She especially enjoyed seeing the kids inside who were so excited to get "ice cream." She'd never been someone who really wanted kids, but lately she thought a lot about her future. Since she had finally left her ex, Becca had thought more and more about where her life was going. Their relationship hadn't been the kind of thing she normally looked for in love, but that was mostly what kept her with him. To her, he was different, he was variety, and he was dangerous. That had been enough for her in the beginning, but after a year of putting up with a man-child, she had grown tired of his antics. After having cared for a ten-year-old trapped in a man's body, she figured that she would be sick of the idea of caring for an actual child, and yet she still found herself admiring their sweet faces and messy cheeks smeared with frozen yogurt.

As she joined the line to get her cup, she noticed the tall frame of the man in front of her. Something about him was very familiar, but she couldn't figure it out exactly. Where had she seen him before? He looked forward almost obstinately, never turning his head back. She tried to sneak a look at his face, but she just couldn't see around his broad frame. Wishing for a chance to strike up a greeting so she could see his face and solve the mystery, she kept her eyes on him. When he took the cups for yogurt, he took two instead of one. Having found her chance, she spoke up: "Could I please have the other cup?" Her stranger turned to her, and she immediately recognized the face of her cute bridge admirer. *Oh, this is turning into my favorite night this week.*

CHAPTER EIGHT

Becca began to wonder if her skywalk admirer had heard her, because he wasn't saying anything. In fact, he looked startled, like she'd jumped out of a dark corner at him. Was there something on her face, or did he always do this when women spoke to him? Thinking he might need to be reminded that she was still waiting, she smiled and offered, "Um... how about that cup?" He looked down at the cups in his hands, seemed to realize he was just standing there like an idiot, and tried to play it off, returning, "Oh, yeah, sorry. Just couldn't let her go. She's a beauty."

She laughed, half at his joke and half at him. Not only was he cute, he was awkward as hell. *Oh he is just what I need tonight,* she cooed to herself, much like a lioness regarding a large field mouse. She probably shouldn't tease him, but she just couldn't stand it. Mockingly studying her cup, she returned with "Huh, I guess it is a pretty good model. You don't see a lot of these around anymore." "Well," he rebutted with a grin, "they have to phase out the old models to make way for the future. The froyo biz is a fast and dangerous game."

This guy was a classic. He had just enough charm mixed with cheesy, stupid jokes to be a thrill for her. Becca wasn't much for the chase of a man, but she liked to be cunning and play with her prey once in a while. She only really ever did it to guys who could make her laugh but didn't know they were doing that well.

Oblivious charm is my one weakness, and this guy is about as oblivious as they come.

The two turned to look at the pumps. She knew exactly what she wanted to get, because she usually just got chocolate with bananas. Variety could be good sometimes, but she loved the stability of her favorite flavor. She could always count on it picking her up from a bad day. Once, she'd tried to add gummi bears. That might have been the worst choice she'd ever made. They never lasted long enough before getting so hard that they were impossible to chew.

"What do you think you'll get?" she asked him. He studied the pumps for a moment, far longer than he should have to for making a simple choice, and answered, "I'm not sure. I don't know what I feel like. I might make a PB&J." She cocked one eyebrow at him: "A peanut butter and jelly sandwich? You can make that?" He turned to her with a dumb smile and chirped, "Sure you can. All you have to do is this." He dashed to the Toppings Bar and began working. He was describing each detail, but she wasn't really listening. Instead, she was watching him. She watched the way he moved, the way he was clearly doing something he loved. He was doing this from memory and by heart. For something so simple and pointless in the vast expanse of life, she was moved for some reason in watching him. *What the hell is wrong with me? It's just frozen yogurt.*

"There, it's done," he yipped, grabbing a colored spoon from the plastic bin. "Now, the best way to eat this is to dip your spoon in and get each layer without mixing or stirring." This was going to suck, and she knew it. *I should probably try it. I don't want to insult him and his crappy yogurt.* She hated trying weird mystery dishes, especially when she had to do so for the satisfaction of others. Still, how bad could it be?

Dipping the spoon into the cup, she pulled a big wad of yogurt out, twirled it to keep from creating a mess, and stuck the whole thing in her mouth. Immediately, she could taste every single thing mixed into the cup. He was right, it tasted exactly like a peanut butter and jelly sandwich. Every single thing about it was perfect. She'd never tasted something so good from this place, and she'd been coming here for months. *He's a goofy little dork, but I think he deserves some praise for this.* "Oh my God, this is fantastic," she moaned, her mouth still full of yogurt. "This tastes just like a PB&J." She didn't need him to admit that this touched him. She could see it all over his face.

Sensing he liked the compliment, and also because it was very true, she continued: "Seriously, this is so good. I can't believe how much this tastes like a peanut butter and jelly sandwich." She started to take another big bite, but he stopped her, putting his hand around her spoon-grasping fist. "Hey, we have to pay for that still," he laughed. She stopped, but not because of his words. She stopped because of his hand. Did she just become excited over his touch? *Ugh, what is wrong with you, Becca? You're an idiot,* she mocked herself in her head. *He made you some frozen yogurt. It's not like he saved your damn cat.*

He took her cup from her and set it down on the scale next to his. The clerk looked to the cups and said, "Are these together?" "Yes," her mystery man answered. She reached into her pocked for her card, warning, "No, you don't have to do that." He put a hand out to her, smiling, and replied, "No, I insist. You complimented my work, and I'll gladly pay for that." He handed the clerk a twenty and, after received the change, dropped the rest in the tip jar. *Okay,* she mused, *he's looking to spend money on you. He'll have to earn that if he wants it that badly.*

He passed her the cup of frozen yogurt, which she received, adding, "Thank you. You didn't have to do that." "I was glad to," he grinned. "Thanks for letting me." They moved out of the line and stood together by the elastic barrier separating the eating area from the line. "What did you make for yourself?" she asked, eyeing his cup. "Oh this isn't much. I felt like something rich, so I made a chocolate covered Oreo," he said before enjoying a hearty spoonful. She grinned and coyly joked, "Do you always come to this froyo shop and woo the ladies with your chef skills?" Just as she had hoped, he coughed, almost choking on his yogurt. She'd caught him off guard. "I uh... don't normally eat here with anyone," he finally sputtered. "I don't believe that," she chuckled. "I bet you wait around here just to buy froyo for unsuspecting ladies, wow them with your skills, and then take them off to your sex dungeon." She was playing her game far more aggressively than usual, but she had a feeling he could take it. She wanted to make him sweat.

He finished his half eaten bite and searched for the words. She could see the nervousness in his eyes. He finally retorted with "I don't have a sex dungeon. I have a two-bedroom apartment." "Ah ha, see?" she grinned, cocking an eyebrow his way. "Already trying to invite me back to your apartment." She could swear there were small beads of sweat on his forehead. This was fun. He was exactly what she needed tonight. Despite her best efforts to maintain her composure, she finally burst with laughter. "Man, you are really fun to tease. Lighten up, guy, I'm just kidding," she joked, playfully punching his shoulder. *God his shoulders are broad,* she found herself thinking. She put a hand out to him and said, "My name's Becca." He took her hand, giving a gentle shake, and added, "I'm Benny."

He really was cute. There was just something about him. He didn't seem terribly sure of himself, but he had this strange natural confidence and stance, even when seated. She'd been around a lot of men in her life, and she'd learned to read them rather well. There was something about him, however, that made it hard to tell if he was actually genuine. Becca began to wonder if she even knew what genuine looked like, and if maybe the reason she couldn't read him as well was because he actually might be.

"Benny, huh?" she grinned, walking past him towards the chairs. "Well it's a pleasure to meet you. Let's sit down. I've been running for a while, and my legs are a little sore." That was a lie, and she knew it. She'd gotten plenty of rest during dinner, but she didn't want to take the chance that he might leave and ruin her fun. Getting him seated guaranteed more conversation, something she'd learned in her work. "Okay," he said, taking the chair next to her. "You were keeping quite a pace earlier." It occurred to her that she hadn't mentioned she remembered him. *Ah, we haven't even covered that he was ogling me. Let's see if I can make him blush.* She widened her eyes a bit to feign recognition and barked, "Oh yes! You're the guy who was standing by the bridge. I was wondering why you looked familiar." She needed a closer, something to tease him with. "You'd think I'd remember your face, considering how you were staring at me."

His face turned a warm, pinkish red, and she knew she'd caught him. He was hoping she wouldn't remember that, but she definitely did. She was having so much fun that she didn't even become annoyed when her phone rang again in her pocket at that moment. She simply tucked her hand in and silenced the call, knowing it was that stupid caller again. When she turned her eyes back to Benny, he had slumped his head down. "Oh, yeah. That's me, the bridge gazer," he moaned beneath a sigh. She realized she had teased him too much. *Throw him a bone, girl.*

"Actually, I was flattered. It's hard to feel attractive when you've been running, sweating and breathing like you're going to die," she giggled, glad to see his face rising with a slight smile. She dug back into her yogurt. "Damn this is good. This is really good." He looked to her with embarrassment, but she made no eye contact with him, knowing that the effect would be much better if she didn't. "I was worried I'd seemed weird," he shrugged. "Oh don't worry, you did," she laughed, "but in cute way. You're cute weird." She could tell right away that he liked hearing that, despite it being a kind of backhanded compliment.

He was different. Though she'd long given up hope of ever experiencing what she called "the ultimate unicorn, a gentleman," she began to wonder if perhaps this guy might actually be one. He wasn't doing anything in particular to make her feel that way. In fact, it was more of a matter of what he wasn't doing. He wasn't ogling her body or trying to hit on her, and he certainly wasn't talking down to her. He seemed to genuinely take interest in her. Then again, she'd been wrong before. If there were one thing she could claim as personal flaw, it would be her taste and history with men. But, in her defense, at least she was consistent.

"So, your name, Becca," he quickly chirped, changing the subject from his predator status, "it's unique. Is it short for anything?" She nodded, signaling that her mouth was far too full of yogurt to speak. Finally, regaining the space, she answered with "Ha, yeah, it's a little odd. My parents named me Rebeccany." He pulled a rather cartoonish double-take. Clearly, he was surprised. "Rebeccany? Really?" he puzzled. "Yeah, they overheard the name once and thought it was beautiful," she clarified. "Personally, it's been a nightmare. Try explaining to anyone why you're not simply named Rebecca. I get it all the time. It's much easier to be called Becca. I prefer it anyway." He grinned, again with that charming, goofy smile of his, and said, "I happen to think it's quite a lovely name."

This guy is asking for it. Nobody charms me, she growled to herself. She rarely let any man charm her, and she certainly never let a man sweep her off her feet. She liked her feet firmly on the ground. *I need to really see what he's expecting here,* she puzzled. Then, it hit her. She knew exactly how to test the waters of his intentions. "God it's hot in here," she moaned, fanning her face. "I mean, sure crank the heat up in an ice cream shop, but still. I need to get this fleece off." He sighed, almost laughing off his relief, and said, "I was hoping you'd say something. I'm burning up in this coat." He reached to pull his left arm out of the sleeve. She waited until he was somewhat awkwardly caught mid-pull and began her routine.

She'd done it a million times, and she knew every move as if they were the beats of her own heart. She reached back with one hand and gently pulled the hair tie gathering her short red hair, feeling it ripple out of the band and fall gently to just the edge of her shoulders. Out of the corner of her eye, she checked her audience. He had completely lost hold of the sleeve and was fumbling to regain his grasp, fixated on her while trying his best to not stare. *Got him.* Moving on to Step Two, she unzipped her fleece, letting the panels fall open to reveal her frame. Becca had always known that she had the natural curves of a full-figured woman, even at her heaviest weight, but there were seldom rare times that she ever glorified her body for the attention of men. This was one of those rare times. She reached behind her to grab her left sleeve and then her right. She knew this arched her back and accentuated her chest and the curves of her torso. That was the point, after all. Though this was all one fluid easy motion, she masterfully took her time, giving him plenty of moments to drink in the whole presentation. As she finished removing the fleece, she gently laid it behind her and gave one final head toss, letting her hair settle. Content that the demonstration had concluded, she turned her eyes back to her captive viewer.

Sure enough, he was caught in his own coat. One would wonder how that could be possible, and yet she'd seen men fall off of walkways or trip on air while staring at her. This guy was certainly disarmed by her looks, and she enjoyed that immensely. There was something more, though. He wasn't drooling or grinning or howling (yes, that had happened too). He was genuinely gazing at her. Gazing. No man had ever gazed at her, and for a moment, she felt her guard dropping in surprise. Seeing Benny's genuine embarrassment wash over his face was just too much, and, unable to contain herself, she burst out laughing. Through her laughs, she giggled, "You okay there, Benny? Need some help?" He seemed to shake off the wonderment and tried to laugh through the discomfort, throwing out all kinds of "Oh, uh, no" and "I can just" with a little "Just let me." At length, he finally gathered his composure and pulled his coat completely off.

Becca wiped a tear of laughter from her eye and tried to regain her own composure. It was then that she noticed the man sitting before her. He was cute, that she knew, but now with his coat off, she had a real chance to look at him. The coat had done an excellent job of hiding his fine, broad shoulders and somewhat muscular chest. He wasn't completely fit, but he certainly seemed to take care of himself. "Well, that's much better," she muttered, sensing the hesitance of her words. Catching herself looking him up and down, she shook herself inside. *What the hell are you doing? Are you eyeing him? The point of this was to see if he drooled over you, not the other way around.* Yet, she couldn't help it. The collar of the coat had hidden the strong, chiseled lines of his jaw and firm neckline. He was such a charming combination of sloppy and well groomed, from his black obsidian hair in a slightly shaggy ear-length cut to his large, muscular hands that looked soft and gentle. God, he was very good looking, and she was not proud to admit that.

Realizing she was probably undressing him with her eyes in a far too obvious manner, she grabbed her yogurt cup and broke the silence asking him about his name. He told her it was a family name and that he'd been marked with it since he was a child. She offered up that he seemed a better fit for the name "Ben." Judging from the grin that washed across his face, she could tell he liked that. The truth was less about how he didn't fit the name and more about how she'd had an ex-boyfriend several years ago named Benny. That relationship hadn't ended well, unless one could consider the act of pawning a ex-lover's belongings that were left in one's apartment (so as to pay off the mountainous cellular phone bill, a bill stemming from thousands of texts, pictures, and calls to other women made by said ex-lover) as a healthy break from a relationship. Becca definitely did not like the name Benny, but she definitely liked Ben, especially this particular Ben.

"So, Ben, what do you do for a living?" she quizzed. As if his words were nothing of importance, he replied, "I'm a PR Consultant for Martin and Glowrey." She wasn't totally savvy to the big shots of the city, but she certainly knew the name of these particular big shots. "Woah, that's a pretty good gig," she teased. "They're quite a name in town. I bet you bring home the big bucks for that." "It's a good job, and the work is really fun," he said with a smile. He carried himself in a way that showed he was professional and proper when he needed to be. That was something Becca envied. She had never learned how to seem well to do, not that she ever needed to or cared to seem that way to others. Still, she had always admired those who knew how to impress by simply looking the part. She could also tell from his clothes that he did well. *That sweater alone must have cost him eighty dollars,* she mused.

He dug his spoon into his cup to take another bite but stopped, dropping the spoon back into the pile of yogurt. "That's a lie," he sighed. "It's not fun. I hate my job." Setting his cup down on the table, he leaned forward, dropping his arms onto his legs. Becca slowly lost the smile from her face. "I've hated my job for a while now. I don't know when it happened, but the magic just kind of disappeared," he said over hushed sighs. "I've just grown tired of the whole thing." She could see that he was genuinely unhappy, and she started to roll her eyes in disgust over such a dramatic turn in her present boy toy, but something stopped her. Maybe it was the fact that she, too, wasn't exactly pleased with her own life. Maybe it was the fact that she didn't really feel so alone when talking to him. *Or, maybe it's the fact that you're getting soft for this guy. Are you kidding me? The last thing you need in your life is some downer talking about how miserable he is. Right? You don't need that, right?*

"That sucks," she offered in a hushed, caring tone. "I'm sorry, Ben. Did something happen to you at work?" "No, not really," he groaned, "and that's kind of the point. Every day is the same. I come in, I browse accounts, I make phone calls, I schedule events and promotions, and I go home. It's the same thing every day. I'm not exactly sure, but I think I'm dead inside." He shuffled his feet before planting them and pushing himself back in the chair.

Dead inside. That was how he described it. She'd never thought of it that way before, but it was perfect. That was exactly how she felt, down to the wire. She felt like her life wasn't going anywhere special, as if it was leading toward an inevitable end. Sure, she was losing weight, she had left her ex, and she was getting her life back together. Still, she felt like something was missing. Though she had new goals for bettering herself, they were short lived. There was nothing keeping her hope alive for a better tomorrow. She needed something or someone to explain to her what one was supposed to look forward to each day.

She stood, grabbing the two cups of yogurt, and tossed them

into the trash by the door. She turned and grabbed her fleece, slipping back into it far more quickly than she had taken to remove it. "Come on," she commanded, "let's go for a walk. You could use it." *So could I.* He smiled, grabbing his coat and rising to meet her. As he pulled his coat back on, she caught herself staring at his chest again. Granted, considering he was taller than her, her gaze naturally fell to his chest. So, that was totally the reason she looked. Definitely.

They stepped out the front door of the shop. He turned and walked a few steps down the street, asking her "Where to?" but she barely heard this. Looking across the street, she noticed a dark grey van parked in a parallel space. She had learned to be observant in her line of work, and she spotted the van the moment they'd hit the door. More than that, she immediately locked eyes with a man, a man she knew very, very well. He was watching them, as was the taller man in the driver's seat. She wasn't interested in talking to them, nor was she interested in finding out what they wanted, but at that very moment, her phone vibrated again. Checking the screen, she saw a single text message: "Are you ready?"

Pocketing her phone and turning back to her new distraction, she rejoined the conversation: "Charm me, Mr. Bigshot. Take me somewhere bright and colorful." "Ha, I'll do my best," he chuckled nervously, "though I don't know where to take you that you haven't seen already." He motioned for her to join him. She skipped to his side and wrapped her arm around his, knowing the driver and passenger of the van could see this exchange. "Lead on," she said with a laugh. He grinned and proceeded to walk her down the street. As they passed shops and offices, she kept an eye on the reflection of the van as it followed them from a typical tracer's distance. This night was definitely interesting.

CHAPTER NINE

As they walked through the city streets, Becca found herself having fun, and this was unexpected. Normally, she was very picky when it came to the company of men. She often liked to tease her boys only to have them go home alone, empty handed after they'd spent the night wining and dining her. Sometimes, usually on Thursdays, she would go out to bars and clubs just to see how many guys would hit on her at the bar. For each of them, she would alternate between her set of histories and back-stories. She loved the thrill of being someone else, her victims never learning the real her.

And yet, here she was with this new guy, and she wasn't lying to him. She certainly wasn't telling him everything, but she was being far more open than her usual operating standard. Maybe she didn't want to be that person anymore, or maybe she just didn't want to be that person to him. *He's not special,* she told herself. *He's just some guy. Why do you care what he thinks?* Yet, the truth was she did, or at least she was considering it. She found herself wondering if he liked her. She then found herself wondering if maybe she wasn't getting enough oxygen to her brain.

There were too many things going through her head. For one thing, she was keeping a constant eye on the van far behind them, making sure it maintained a safe distance. She was having a good time, and she was in no mood to deal with the two men driving. She'd had enough of their company in her past, and she was eager to move on from that life. As a matter of fact, she found herself very eager to move on from her entire life currently. Being around Ben made her consider her own life and circumstances. It was as if he had revealed her desire for a kindred spirit, or at least someone that understood her recent upswing of depression. He really made her feel less alone.

As they walked, she kept him talking, asking him more about his job and the people with which he did business. She liked hearing about his best and worst clients, but she especially enjoyed the stories of high profile meetings and events that had embarrassing outcomes. He seemed to have plenty of stories, and since the subject kept any attention off of her personal life, she was more than glad to discuss it. When they passed by a building he had a story connected with, they would pause while he regaled her with his big shot life. He laughed and often commented that his stories were silly and pointless, but she reminded him that, if she were bored, she'd tell him to shut up. He always grinned when she said that.

Their pointless meandering through the streets and square led them to the park. After their laughter settled from one of his most embarrassing stories, Benny dried his eyes from laughter and asked, "So, Becca, where do you work?" This was a subject she had hoped they wouldn't visit. Maybe that's why she kept asking about his job. She wasn't proud of what she did, and she hated the work. Lately, she wanted more and more to shake her old life and start from scratch. Her life wasn't glamorous like his, and she certainly wasn't respectable. "Oh," she finally answered after a pause that may or may not have been an hour long, "I work from home. I sell things online." "Ah, I see, a private business owner. Such a glamorous life," he teased. "Hey, shut up, Big Bucks," she barked, elbowing him. "It pays the bills."

He laughed, rubbing his ribs. "Hey, take it easy, killer. So, what do you sell? Do you have a product?" "No, not like that," she replied, searching for the right words. "I sell things online for other people." She continued to explain, but the words felt wrong to her. She wanted to sound reputable and respectable, but she wasn't and she knew that. There were very few things in life of which Becca felt ashamed, but her past occupational history was definitely one of those things. She'd never held a good job in her life, and she'd certainly cheated employers many times. She had to admit, however, that she was making her job sound pretty good so far. "Ah, you're more of a dealer. That seems like an interesting business," he said, rubbing his chin and grinning. "I'd imagine there's money to be made doing that." She laughed and crossed her arms. "I do pretty well for myself. The trick is to make yourself seem more valuable than you really are." He smiled, "I'm sure you have no trouble seeming valuable to people." She felt the heat behind her cheeks and realized she was actually blushing.

Ugh, I just want to punch him, she growled in her head. *He's so stupidly charming. Why did I ever decide to go anywhere with him? This is going to blow up in my face.* Then again, why did she care if it did? He was nothing to her. He was just some guy she had met. *I bet he's got some high class girlfriend who spends all his money for him,* she laughed to herself, though she was aware of the slight tinge of jealousy in this thought. "So," she asked him, turning the subject, "you make all that good money, but do you have anyone to share it with?" He coughed, apparently caught off guard, "Oh, uh, yes. I have a girlfriend named Karen." She immediately hated her. "Ah, I bet she's a classy uptown lady," she said with attempted sincerity that barely masked the sarcasm in her voice. He scoffed with a laugh: "Yeah, she's pretty great. She likes to think herself an uptown lady, but I think she truly..." His phone rang in his pocket. A look of sudden awareness and alarm crossed his face, and he quickly retrieved his phone.

"It's her. Let me take this, and I'll be right back." He smiled like he wasn't uncomfortable, but she knew better. She tried to ignore the jealous feeling that seemed to be welling up inside her and turned her attention away from him. This interruption gave her a chance to better scan for the tailing stalkers. She scanned the views of the street as best she could, but she didn't see any signs of the dark grey van. When they had entered the park, she had led them away from the street running parallel. She knew the van wouldn't be able to follow them as well. Hopefully, the two men in the van would lose them and give up, though she highly doubted that. After all, they'd hired her for a reason, and they certainly weren't the kind who gave up easily. She detested micro-management, and these two were the kings of it, especially the shorter passenger in the van. She'd had more than enough of him trying to control her operations, let alone her life.

While she tried to plan a way to escape the park without being spotted, she tried her best to not listen in to his conversation with his girlfriend. She definitely wasn't listening to him attempting to talk with his girlfriend while she seemingly rambled on and on. She also wasn't listening to him tell his girlfriend what he was doing that night. *Wait,* she stopped suddenly. *Did he just say he was with a guy? Did he lie to her? He did. He just lied to her.* She definitely wasn't smiling. She was certainly not grinning and wondering what he was doing later tonight. *Ugh, okay, now you're definitely an idiot,* she told herself.

He hung up the phone and came back to where she stood. "Sorry about that," he sighed, rubbing his neck. "She wanted to talk for a while." "I know, I heard," she laughed, cocking one eyebrow. "Please, tell me more about this guy you met. I'm sure he was a really great guy." His face turned a warm red, and he hung his head with a groan. "Oh, you heard that," he sighed. "Yep, and I must say, I had hoped that I don't look very manly. Maybe I need to run more," she joked, rubbing her stomach and ribs. "I'm sorry," he said with a groan, "She can be very jealous, and I didn't want her freaking out." She grinned, stepping closer to him. "It's okay. I like the scandal of it." She took his arm again, and they walked under the archway and further into the park.

They wandered through the park, and she was surprised that she wasn't bored yet. Anyone offering to take her on a moonlit stroll would usually have her hailing a cab and calling it quits for the night, but she just couldn't stop having fun with Ben. She also couldn't believe how open she was still being with her life. She wasn't used to someone asking questions about her the way he did. He wanted to know so much about her. Normally, men wanted to ask her stupid questions about her measurements, her favorite drink, or if she was into some band, movie, tv show, or some other thing that might give them a shot with her. These were questions she tolerated and sometimes even enjoyed, given the right mood. He wasn't asking those questions, however. He asked her where she grew up, where she went to school, and where she wanted to go in life. She was somewhat reserved to answer these, as she rarely shared her personal life with anyone. Her ex hadn't even asked her these kinds of things, excepting rare occasions where the two had been intimate. She both hated and enjoyed this new guy's curiosity.

The conversation turned to the park itself. They discussed their favorite parts and places of the park, with him having more knowledge of the area than her. She let him tell her the history and secrets of places he knew about, not necessarily because she cared, but because she liked seeing the passion he had for this in his face. He was clearly a history nerd, and that was a characteristic she rarely found in other people. She loved the History Network, and she often made time to visit historic places wherever she went, but she never discussed this with anyone. To her, this was a personal trait that she enjoyed hiding from the world. She could retreat to a museum or hall and enjoy being taken to another time. Perhaps that's what brought her to her current line of work.

Benny stopped walking and paused. He turned to her with a gleam in his eye. "Come on," he tugged at her. "I want to show you something." She followed him past a line of fences and the small amphitheater to a cluster of trees off to a corner of the park. "Duck your head, it's just over here," he warned, bending and helping her to sneak under the tree line with him. When she finally stood, she found herself standing in a small patch of grass and mulch with a large oak tree at one end. "This is my spot," he said, giving a goofy sweeping motion with his hand as if he'd laid out a red carpet for her. *This guy is so adorably nerdy. I should keep him for a while, like a house cat.* "I come here when I need to be alone, or when I need to think," he explained. "I found it one day while throwing a Frisbee with my cousin from Georgia." She smiled. He had brought her somewhere private, somewhere he didn't share with the world. In a way, she felt like he opened himself up to her. She walked to the oak tree and sat down in the dry mulch by its roots. Looking up to him, she patted the mulch next to her. He grinned and joined her.

She turned her head away from him. That's when she saw it: the skyline. She'd never really looked at the city lights and the skyline from this angle. The whole thing looked like a fresh oil painting. The moon hanging over the skyscrapers cast a beautiful silver glow against the cool lines of glass and steel. The sight was simply breathtaking. She couldn't believe she hadn't seen this before. She also couldn't believe she cared. Shouldn't she be telling him how dorky this was, how weird he was for sitting here alone? Why did she think this was romantic? Why the hell was she enjoying this so much? This wasn't something she did. She was cool and aloof and all that. She didn't sit beneath trees with boys and gaze at the moon.

"This is a pretty great spot," she sighed, giving in to her enjoyment. "You get to see a lot of wonderful things." She scooted a little closer to him, telling herself that this was simply because she was just a little cold. "Yeah, the lights weren't on when I first found the place," he said with a grin. "I only saw them by chance one night when I came here. I make it a tradition to come here at least once a month and see the lights, though that's really best spent during the fall and winter months." They sat there together, neither of them speaking, just staring up at the lights and the moon. Somewhere in that time, she realized she had laid her head on his shoulder. *Well, I can't just jerk my head away now. I'll just keep it there so I don't hurt his feelings. I wouldn't want to be rude or cruel,* she lied to herself.

"Thank you for bringing me here," she said, breaking the silence. "I needed this tonight. I've been so stressed out with work, and I just needed a chance to unwind and relax." He gave a small sigh of contentment and said, "My pleasure. I'm glad someone else can appreciate this place, especially when you're stressed out." She chuckled and said, "I really shouldn't be. My job is easy, and I shouldn't get so worked up about it. Maybe that's not what upsets me. Maybe it's just the nature of my job. Maybe it's my life right now." He turned to her and asked, "What do you mean? Don't you like selling things for people? That seems like a fun, entertaining business." She paused, taking a long breath. He wouldn't understand her life or the things she'd done, but maybe he could understand some of it. "It is, and it isn't," she began. "It's not the kind of job you want forever. I don't really want it at all, to be honest. Lately, I feel lost. I feel like I'm not doing anything with my life." She didn't say it, but she thought to herself that she felt like life didn't want anything to do with her. She'd thought that for a while.

She sat up, pulling her legs up to her and grasping her knees with her arms. "I didn't think I'd doing this still, and I just, I don't know, I thought I'd be someone else. I just thought life would go a different way, and I know that I'm only twenty-eight, but I thought I'd be on my way to my future by now, whatever the hell it's supposed to be." He, too, sat up, turning completely towards her. "I know exactly what you mean," he replied, putting a hand on her shoulder. He looked at her with a kind of compassion she hadn't seen in a very long time. "I hate my life. I hate my job, I hate my apartment, and I hate this city. I treasure places like this because they make me forget how miserable I am. And that's the problem, because I have a fantastic job and a great apartment. I have a relationship that makes me happy, at least most of the time. But lately, I feel lost. I feel like I don't belong, like I don't matter." For the first time that night, she saw herself in him. She saw the same tormented person, scratching at the surface of things and trying to find the answers. He was just like her. As he continued talking, she heard him, but it seemed like the words were her own, not his. It was then that she felt herself getting close to him. She was caring about him, maybe even wanting him in a deeper way than just a one-night stand.

"I have to tell someone something, and I think it should be you," he said in a hushed tone. She could see that he was nervous, and she wanted to comfort him, but she had no idea how to do so. "Tonight, here in this spot, I was going to kill myself." She didn't speak. She couldn't, for fear that her words would break him in to a million pieces. She knew she was staring at him with her mouth agape, but she couldn't stop. "Here?" she finally asked, having nothing else that felt right to say. "Yes, Becca. I was so miserable. I didn't want to live another minute, and I planned on killing myself. I chose to do it here, under my favorite tree." She suddenly felt like she was tarnishing this sacred place. "Is that why you brought me here?" "No," he replied. "I never intended to tell you any of this. I couldn't do it. When the time came, I just couldn't do it."

Her heart broke for him. He was such a sweet guy, and yet he couldn't see that. "Why?" she begged. "Why would you kill yourself?" The question seemed fair, but she knew it wasn't. Who was she to question his motives? Deep in her heart, she knew she'd thought of the same thing. Suicide had been an option for her, whether she admitted it or not. He was talking to her now, but she wasn't able to listen. She just kept thinking about Benny and about ending it all. Sometimes, it felt like the only thing she could do that was her own choice.

She broke from the haze of her own thoughts to find him digging into his pocket. He pulled his hand from the pocket, his hand that contained a pistol. She knew the make and model of the pistol almost immediately, another trait of her life she wished she could just forget. *He does not deserve to be hurt. He doesn't deserve this kind of pain. I would never forgive myself if I hurt him.* Then, far in the distance, she heard it: the sound of the van starting up. She knew the sound immediately, and she remembered who had been following them. The hairs on the back of her neck rose in alert, and she felt a cold chill of realization wash over her. "I shouldn't have done this," she muttered. "I shouldn't be here." She looked about herself, wishing she could simply disappear and teleport to her apartment. Hopefully she could somehow still leave him and protect him. She knew they were looking for her, and they were expecting her to deliver on her promise.

"No, it's okay," he quickly stammered, stuffing the gun back into his coat pocket. "I'm not going to kill myself. I don't think so. I just… it's okay. I won't. Just calm down." Becca barely heard his words. They were faint in her ears. She was already thinking of the danger she'd put him in. She had to run. She couldn't stay near him. He didn't belong in her life, at least not like this. "I need to leave you," she muttered through rushed breaths. "You don't need to be around me. I'll only hurt you and make this worse."

She stumbled toward the tree line, ducking beneath the branches. He reached out to her, begging her: "Wait, I promise. I won't do this. I didn't mean to scare you. Just come back." She paused at the trees, looking back at him. She wanted to tell him that he wasn't scaring her. She tried to, searching for words that would make him realize, but there were no words that would be enough. She gave him a smile and dashed away.

She wanted to tell him so much. She wanted to explain to him why she had to run. There was just too much to tell. How could she have been so stupid as to think that she could bring someone like him into her life? There was no room for him in her world. He was far too good a person to be entrenched in the curse of her company. She needed to be alone. She belonged alone, at least for now. He was a nice guy, maybe even a great guy, though, truth be told, she wasn't really sure exactly what a great guy would be like. He was the nearest thing to a good man in her life, but she knew that he couldn't be a part of her world. At that moment, her phone vibrated with a text message. She looked down at the screen and saw that it was from the same number as before. "Is he the mark?" She felt her throat tighten, as if she might vomit.

As she made her way across the grounds, she tried to never look back for the van. She hoped that they would either lose interest or simply follow her back to her apartment. That was where she was going, and she was fairly certain they would think of that too. She could handle them. They were no danger to her, but him? They could ruin his life. She couldn't bring that upon him.

As she passed through Market Place, heading closer to her street, she began to worry about him. What if he chose to end his life? Would she be the cause? She shook her head, trying to rid herself of the worry and concern for him. *First off, he's just one guy. He's not the end of the world,* she growled to herself. *Second off, so what if he does? He's nothing to you. You don't even know him.* She tried to pretend that this second thought didn't horrify her. She also tried to pretend that she wasn't going to cry if she found out he had actually killed himself.

The street was dark, with barely anyone around. Night fell so much earlier at this time of the year, and she rarely stayed out late if she could help it. Granted, the majority of her work was best done in the evening, but she tried to stay indoors at night. The city wasn't exactly known as a crime hot spot, but she knew some of the rougher characters that lived in the area. As she turned onto her street, she realized she was completely out of breath and was wheezing. She stopped, falling into the brick wall next to her, trying to catch her breath. In between breaths, she paused, trying to listen for the sounds of the van's engine. Somewhere, faintly, she could hear the engine sputtering and growling, like a monstrous creature that had picked up her scent. In a way, she hoped they had, because that meant they would leave him alone. With any luck, they wouldn't think another thing of him and let him go his way.

Regaining her composure, she dashed to the door of her stoop. Her apartment sat at the top of a small housing block about two blocks from Market Place. She chose the apartment because it had roof access and was the highest available apartment in the neighborhood. She loved to go and sit on the roof, looking up at the stars and the city lights. She actually found herself jealous that she couldn't see the skyline view the way she had in his private spot. Still, the place had charm and style. She darted up the stairs, digging into the waistband pocket of her track pants. Pulling out a small door key, she quickly thrust the key into the lock. She turned the key, but the door would not budge. *Damn it. Why now, of all times? I should have had this lock fixed months ago.* The lock finally rolled back in the chamber, and she burst through her door, locking it behind her.

Secure in the knowledge that she had reached home and would be safe, she collapsed against her door. Her night hadn't gone exactly as she had wanted, and she began to rethink everything. She still smiled, thinking about Benny's goofy charm and gentle grace. "Ugh, stupid Ben. I'm actually going to miss him," she sighed aloud to no one. The welcoming cries of her cat, Cheddar, could be heard echoing from the kitchen. Cheddar strolled into the room as if sensing she needed a friend. He rubbed against her outstretched legs, purring almost immediately upon his arrival. She looked down at her feline friend, his fat round face looking back at her. He had a way of staring directly at her with those big, wide "moon eyes" and making her feel loved immediately.

Picking him up gently, she pulled him close to her chest, scratching behind his ears and on his chin. "Why don't I ever get a good guy, Cheddar?" she asked, half to him and half to herself. "Well, at least I have one good man in my life." She tussled his fur and ears, and he let out a soft call of agreement. He started to curl up in her legs, but she lifted him up while she stood. "Hang on there, buddy. I just got home. Give a girl some space," she laughed, kissing him on the forehead. He wove himself around her neck and perched on her shoulders, giving a lick on her cheek as if to signify she could begin walking.

With her feline companion now draped around her neck, she wandered through the room to the kitchen. "You're probably just being lovey-dovey because you're hungry," she said in a mocking tone. "You only ever treat me this way when you want food." Stooping at the kitchen counter, she cocked her shoulders at an angle, allowing him to step off onto to the counter. She turned to the cabinet by the microwave and dug out a can of cat food. The can advised that a fully-grown cat should have a half a can at most, but that seemed like far too little food for Cheddar. "A growing boy needs his nourishment," she whispered to him, as if there was anyone in the room who might object. After popping the top of the can off and scooping the contents out into his dish, she gave Cheddar a scratch behind the ears and left him to his meal.

She returned to the living room, flopping down onto the couch. Her apartment was of modest size, though some could argue it was fit for a king. She had lived by herself even when she and her ex had been together. She was never one for sharing space with another person, usually because she couldn't stay in a relationship for longer than a year, and a year was being generous. Her relationships were more like summer flings than actual emotional commitments. She loved her space and privacy. The closest she had ever come to living with someone was her ex, and that was simply because she had told him where she hid the key outside the door. Her apartment door had a small window above it, and the sill of the window made for a perfect hiding spot for a small key.

"Ugh, too tired to change clothes," she groaned. "I'll do it later. I need something to take my mind off of tonight." She turned on her DVR and skimmed through the shows captured from earlier broadcast. Settling on a crime drama, she propped a pillow up for her head and curled up to enjoy her show. Within five minutes, she was out cold. She woke occasionally, especially if the show's volume level rose for any reason, but she was never awake longer than a moment at best. That was probably the best explanation for the next hour's events being such a blur.

Somewhere, within the hour's time, she woke to find the two men lifting her off the couch. Before she could scream, a gag was tied over her mouth, and her hands were tied behind her. She could only assume the two had found the key over the door. She never should have left it there. She struggled, but they were simply too strong. Throwing a black hood over her head, they secured the hood at her neck with what sounded like a zip tie.

From there, she tried to keep a clear head as they carried her downstairs. She knew screaming was useless, and she certainly wouldn't be reasoning with them, especially the shorter man. Feeling them leading her to the van, she barely struggled when they put her in the back. They were gentle with her, clearly trying their best not to hurt her. As she sat down by the van doors, she heard and felt the presence of another person in the back. Assuming this other captive was subdued just like her, communication would be fruitless and futile. Resigning to her current fate, she laid her head back against the cold walls of the van. This was certainly one interesting night.

CHAPTER TEN

Benny and Becca sat on the edge of the van's bed, their hands bound by the thick cable ties. The two men smiled at their captives, though Benny found nothing about them to be worthy of smiling. Both were human tanks. The shorter man stood roughly 6'6", and his chest might have been as big around as Benny's whole body. The other man, looming stoically next to the first, stood at least half a foot taller than his counterpart. He, too, was built like a locomotive. There would be no running or attempts to flee. The two men blocked any chance of escape by simply standing beside each other. They literally formed a human wall.

Finally, breaking the short silence and coming to his senses, Benny stammered through a series of queries, asking Becca if she were okay and if they had hurt her and if she were okay again and what they wanted and who they were. Finally, the shorter man reached out and slapped Benny across the face. "My, he is quite the chatter box. Now I regret not leaving him gagged," he laughed. Becca snarled at the short man, "You leave him alone. He doesn't concern you. Let him go." "Oh, well, in that case, let me hail a taxi and have him on his way," the short man chuckled. "I do apologize, good sir, for inconveniencing you. After all, Ms. Becca is clearly the commanding officer of our small army. My life is but to serve her every wish." Becca spit at him, but he stepped to one side. "How repugnant, darling. You're far too attractive for spitting."

"I told you already: he isn't involved in any of this. He has no part in your stupid plan," she barked. "Oh come now, dearest," the short man said with a chuckle. "Do you honestly expect me to believe that he is just a 'friend' of yours? You don't have friends." "What do you want with us, Demi?" she asked through gritted teeth. "What do I want? Why, I simply want you to be an honorable woman of your word. I want you to finish the job," he said, grinning and crossing his arms. Benny turned a puzzled head to her and asked, "Do you know these thugs?" "Sir, you insult us. We are not mere 'thugs.'" Demi replied. Becca sighed and shook her head gently. "I... we..." she began, but paused to find the right words. "This is Demi, and that rock monster behind him is his brother Ronni. And yes, I do know them. I have worked for them." "Oh come now, must we hide what we have, chéri?" Demi pouted. He grinned at Benny and spoke with a kind of snake-like hiss: "Ms. Becca does indeed work for us, but she and I are also lovers."

"Like hell we are. I'm through with you. I told you that last month, and I haven't changed my mind." "Your words pierce my heart and shatter my soul," he said, clutching his chest and feigning injury.

Benny's eyes widened. "Wait, you're the Tzetki brothers?" "At your service," Demi replied, removing an invisible cap and bowing. Benny's mouth fell open. He hadn't lived in the city long, but he'd lived there long enough to know that crime had become a bit of a problem. There were two bit thugs and crooks, and then there were "crime bosses." The evening news had begun to use that phrase quite affectionately, and the Tzetkis were definitely the most popular name on that list of crime. Of course, no investigation or case had ever turned up enough evidence to tie the Tzetkis to any illegal activity, but that might have been the reason they had risen in popularity and fame. They seemed like celebrities.

At that very moment, the thought occurred to Benny that

there must be a simple reason why no one ever catches the Tzetkis in their crimes. He wanted to believe it was because they had a kind of silver screen magic at evading the police, that they always rode off into the night while the police stood looking foolish. He knew, though, that the truth was much more serious and grim: they were never caught because there were never witnesses. Benny was in real danger, and it looked as though he would probably get his wish for death. In that moment, Benny felt fear welling up inside him, the kind of fear that a child feels when faced with an unknown terror. But there was something else. He wasn't just afraid. There was another emotion, one that almost masked the fear. For a moment, he thought it might have been panic, but then he realized exactly what he was feeling: he was excited. In a strange way, and far from anything he'd ever experienced before, he found this moment of danger and uncertainty to be exciting.

Benny's eyes grew wide, and he finally whispered, "Wow, the Tzetkis." Demi put a hand to his chest. "Ronni, our reputation precedes us. Would you like an autograph, my friend? If you have some paper and a pen, I'm happy to oblige. Ms. Becca, I can sign your chest if you like." "Go to hell," Becca growled. "Just tell me what you want from us." Demi signed and rubbed his temples. "Becca, dearest, I've already told you: I want you to finish what you promised. I want you to complete the task at hand." Becca stood and started toward him, but Ronni pushed her back to sitting on the van bed floor. "No, you stay. Do not move," he thundered, his voice low and powerful. "I've already told you, I'm not doing this anymore. I don't want any part of it. I'm through working for you," she groaned. "Love, you do not simply walk away from me. Not only is it insulting and dishonorable, it's frankly quite stupid." He stepped forward and leaned down to her face. She winced ever so slightly, and Benny wasn't sure if she feared being struck or if the very placement of his face next to hers made her ill. His lips curled into a harsh grin, and he muttered, "You do not tell Demi Tzeki 'no.'"

Benny wanted to break the tension, to shake the scene and

put her at ease. He didn't know what to say, but he knew that if ever there was a time for him to be tough and brave, now was that time. After what seemed like an hour of searching for the right words, Benny finally gathered his courage and, in the strongest voice he could muster, declared, "Hey, leave her alone." Everyone collectively turned to him, each wearing a surprised look as if to ask if he had really said that. Demi rose to an upright position, walked over to Benny, and slapped him across the face again. Judging from the looseness of his hit, Benny figured the slap wasn't meant to wound him. "That, my good man, is for thinking you have any ounce of authority over myself or my brother. What role you shall play in this evening remains to be seen, but I do hope that you are more than refuse of which we shall have to dispose." Demi had a way of grinning that both made him seem charming and yet completely psychotic, and Benny was certain that no one had ever made him more uncomfortable.

Ronni turned his eyes to the moon. Still looking at the night sky, he said, "Brother, night is short. We do not have time for this." Demi crossed his arms and pouted. "Oh, very well. I can't help it if I enjoy playing with my food. Now then, let's move on to business. Ronni, be a good lad and bring our friends." Ronni lumbered over to the two captives and lifted them to their feet. Using a rather large folding knife, he cut the restraints from their hands. Benny shot a look of concern to Becca, but she was not looking at him. She kept her eyes on Demi, watching him as he walked to the edge of what appeared to be a grass embankment. Ronni gently pressed their backs, and the two walked to where Demi stood.

The barely present crescent moon cast little to no light on the scene before them. The low hills of the valley appeared to be coated in a fine grey powder, and the roads were barren. The only light came from the few external lights mounted on the sides of what appeared to Benny to be a very large warehouse. The entrance to the warehouse was illuminated by a single hanging light, casting an almost perfect half-circle of light around the rolling metal door. Benny couldn't be certain, but the place appeared to be a packing warehouse. There were no more than three box trailers parked at the building, and with no light shining on the sides, he couldn't make out to whom they belonged. Benny also took note of the fact that the warehouse was gravely silent, and, apart from an old Pontiac sedan, there didn't seem to be any signs of employees still working this late.

Demi propped his leg up on a rock by the embankment and stared down at the warehouse. He turned his head just enough to show his grin over his shoulder. "I believe you two know this place." Becca groaned and hung her head, but Benny replied, "Um, I don't." Demi turned his head to Benny and raised his eyebrows. "You're joking. Surely that's a joke." "No," Benny replied, trying to mask his unease at being the odd man out, "I don't have any idea where we are." Demi shook his head and rubbed his temples. "Well, drat. I had hoped we were all on the same page with this. I detest exposition," he moaned, but he raised an arm and cleared his throat. "My friend, I welcome you to the Such-A-Tees main distribution center."

Demi paused, letting the sound of his words echo across the embankment and down to the walls of the warehouse. He grinned, watching Benny's face, but his grin began to subside. "You're not overcome with surprise and wonderment." Benny looked around the lot and said, "I'm sorry. I just..." Demi stepped toward Benny and gestured broadly at the warehouse. "Oh come on, surely you've heard of us. We are the biggest supplier of high demand clothing for the young, hip, culturally relevant consumer." He waited for Benny to respond, but Benny said nothing. "Oh for God's sake..." Demi cut himself short. He gathered his composure, paused, looked at Benny and, accentuating every word, said, "We make people cool."

Demi cleared his throat and turned back to his post by the rock. He put his foot back up on the rock. "Now then, as I was saying," he began, but he paused. "Damn it, this simply doesn't feel as grand anymore," he said, and he took his foot from the rock. He shot a glare at Benny, and Benny, not really knowing what to say, simply muttered a meek "Sorry." Demi hung his head and pinched the bridge of his nose, massaging it gently. "Never mind, never mind. Let's just move on."

He turned his attention back to the warehouse below and cleared his throat once again. "You see, my friend, my dear brother and I are silent controlling members of the leadership of this enterprise. We saw an opportunity to further our ventures and stepped in on the ground floor. In doing so, we have fashioned ourselves a front for the movement of our investments and capital." Becca groaned in irritation and said to Benny, "He's so full of shit. These two bought into the company so that they'd have a front for illegal business. They ship and receive illegal items from here. It's their little 'Boys Club.'" Demi stopped his prideful posing and turned back to Becca. "You ruin all joy. You know that, right?" Before Becca could reply with a snide comment, Benny chimed in: "I had gathered as much. I assume that none of the other owners are aware of your operations?" Demi grinned and replied, "What they do not know has thus far not killed them."

Still grinning, Demi continued: "Here is where Ms. Becca's role, and, by association, yours as well, comes into play. We have received a shipment of goods for immediate sale inside the warehouse. The items are currently nestled between two stacks of new 100% cotton shirts, ready for delivery. We need our goods removed from that shipment container and placed in this vessel." At this, Ronni threw a black duffle bag down on the ground by Becca's feet. "We would do this ourselves, but, as you can imagine, it simply would not do for us to be seen removing our nefarious wares on our own property. Also, we plan on making an insurance claim to recoup losses from this rather costly transaction. Thus, we would greatly appreciate your assistance in this, and there will certainly be a reward for your cooperation."

Demi turned back to look at the warehouse and directed their attention to a far door barely lit by a single canopy light. "Ms. Becca will enter behind that front door. There is a window on the second floor that does not close properly, and so it is often left unlocked." Ronni chuckled and said, "It does not help that I break window jam a week ago." "Yes, my dear brother provided us an access point, and so we shall use it. Or rather, you will." Becca was growing more and more impatient. Her gripping fingers were creating small channels in her arms as she tried to restrain her anger. Finally, she burst, barking, "There's no damn way I'm doing this. I told you I'm done, and I'm sick of being your little pet. This is a stupid operation, and it's sloppy at best. You two can go to Hell."

Ronni started to reach for Becca, presumably to fold her into some kind of pretzel or human balloon animal, but Demi gently placed his palm on his brother's chest. "I do see your trepidations, and I understand your discomfort about the matter," he said, taking slow, methodical steps toward her. "That being said, I do believe you will see that this is the best course of action for you and your compatriot. I would recommend that you not refuse this offer." "I'd recommend that you shove your head up your ass. Did you not hear me? I'm through talking this over. I'm not doing it, and neither is Ben," said Becca, and her eyes clearly punctuated her declaration.

Demi's face began to run the gamut of reddish hues, slowly billowing with rage and anger. He stormed to the van and threw a hard right jab at the side, producing a rather sizable dent. The body of the van rocked an inch to the side, enough to knock one of the doors shut. "Damn you, you miserable harlot," Demi snarled. "Why do you always ruin the things I love? Do you honestly think you are anything without me?" He turned his burning gaze to her, his face almost sweating from the heat of his anger. "You are nothing without my existence. The very words I speak should be sweet nectar for your miserable, pathetic soul. I gave you everything you have. I gave you a new life, a better life, you pathetic little maggot." He charged forward, marching like a great predator closing in on hapless prey. He raised his hand, aligning it with Becca's face. Benny knew exactly what he was going to do next, and he couldn't and wouldn't let that happen.

As Demi closed the gap between the van and Becca, Benny

stepped confidently between the two of them. Granted, Benny was terrified. Demi clearly was ready to strike, and he didn't look like he was holding back this time. Still, Benny would never let him hit her, and he was prepared to fight if need be. Benny stood directly in front of Becca and shrouded her with his body. Demi raised his hand higher but stopped. Something was stopping him from attacking; Benny could see that. He almost barked some kind of stupid command, like, "Get away," or "Don't make me hurt you," but he, too, stopped mid-thought. It was then that Benny felt the firm grasp on his arm. Becca was squeezing his arm, and rather tightly at that. He turned to look at her, and he could see in her eyes a swirling mix of rage and fear. Becca wasn't a weak woman by any means, but it was clear that Demi scared her. There was something else, though. Benny couldn't be sure of it, but as Becca turned her eyes to Benny's, he could almost believe that he saw joy in her eyes. She seemed to be comforted by Benny's arm, by Benny's body before hers, by the man himself. Then, when he turned back to Demi, he could see that Demi wasn't looking at Benny. He'd been looking at Becca. Even now, as he slowly lowered his arm, he kept his eyes on her white-knuckled hands.

"You can't be serious," Demi chuckled. "This one? Really? Of all the men in the city, you choose this one?" Becca tried to speak, but no words came to her lips. Demi let out a kind of surprised coughing laugh, as if the very thought had stolen the air from his lungs. "You were supposed to care for only me. This wasn't the point of it all. You were never meant to care for the…" Demi stopped himself mid-thought. His eyes grew wider, and a smile began to run across his face. He turned to his brother and said, "Ronni, bring the bag. We're going down to the shop." Ronni looked at his brother, looked at the bag, and then down to the warehouse. "Yes. Wait. No?" "Ronni," Demi cooed, "be a dear and grab the black bag. Trust me. We are still in business."

Ronni knelt down and snatched the black duffel bag from the ground. Demi walked to the back of the van and grabbed something, though Benny could not make out what it was. For a moment, he considered telling Becca to run. They weren't bound at their feet, and they could easily get over a few of these hills before tiring. Ronni, however, looked like he could eat these hills, and Benny wasn't really interested in finding out how fast he was either. Benny also couldn't take the chance that one of the two men had a gun. He wouldn't be surprised if Demi was getting one out of the van at that very moment. *There has to be something that I can do to get Bec-,* Benny thought, but he cut himself short. Benny had suddenly remembered that he, too, had a gun, and for some reason it hadn't been taken from him yet. *Why wouldn't they take my gun? You know what? It doesn't matter,* Benny said to himself, trying not to grin. *I have to protect Becca. As soon as I can, I'm ending this.*

Demi closed the van doors and locked them. Turning back to his brother, he said, "Let's see, do we have everything? The product carrier, my right hand man, and our esteemed colleague: yes, everything is here. I suppose we're ready to go." Becca snarled, "We're not going anywhere. I already told you that. I'm done talking." Demi reached into the waistband of his pants and removed a rather large pistol from behind his back. Benny had no idea what kind of pistol it was, but it was certainly the largest handgun he'd ever seen. "Why, of course, my dear," Demi said with a sigh, "we are certainly done talking. There is no more discussion to be had. There is simply the job at hand, and you will certainly complete your job." Becca laughed. "Oh please, you won't shoot me. What a stupid threat." Demi frowned, pointed the gun at her feet, and fired three times. The gun's discharge was deafening, but it certainly got the message across. "As I said," Demi said through gritted teeth, "you're finishing the job."

With that, Demi led the group to the edge of the embankment. "Well, who's up for going first? Anyone? Do we have a volunteer?" He looked among the three of them for a moment, and then turned his attention to Benny. "You, sir. Please, a round of applause for our volunteer," he said, grabbing Benny by the arm and leading him to the edge. "Right, off with you then," he said, shoving him in the back.

CHAPTER ELEVEN

Benny lay at the foot of the embankment, stunned by the tumble he had just taken down the short dirt hill. The others stood above him looking down. Demi snickered and said, "Oh, dear. I should have mentioned the dirt, as it is rather soft and loose. Do be careful everyone." Benny gathered himself and stood up, dusting off his jacket. By the time he had come to his senses, everyone had made their way down the embankment by following the path set by Demi. Benny dusted himself once more and felt a small pile of dirt in his coat pocket. Before he could empty the pocket, he felt the gun pressed into his back. "You are clean enough, pretty boy," Demi growled. "Walk."

The party continued on to the front door of the warehouse. Demi reached for the door but stopped abruptly. "You know, we really shouldn't leave the possibility of being seen like this to chance. Ronni, be a dear and adjust the lighting." Ronni grinned and reached down to pick up a palm-sized rock. He looked to Benny and Becca, motioning for them to back up. Before they could step back more than two feet, Ronni hurled the rock at the floodlight hanging far above the front door. The bulb of the floodlight burst into a shower of glass and flashing light, raining the shards down upon the ground. Benny coughed a laugh and said, "Wow, good throw." Ronni grinned a little more and bowed ever so slightly.

"Thank you, dear brother. That's much better," Demi said, and he opened the front door. The echo of the opening door rolled down the long space of the warehouse. As the four walked into the open warehouse, Benny was surprised by the space before them. The building certainly looked sizable outside, but the inside was incredible. The walls seemed to stretch forever, and the giant racks towered over them, easily twenty feet high. Each rack stood three rows tall, holding any number of pallets loaded with boxes. The top rack row of boxes were wrapped tightly in plastic, while the bottom row held pallets with loosely stacked boxes. The whole place had a kind of crude, machine smell mixed with the warm scent of freshly washed linen.

The warehouse had very little lighting currently in use, apart from a few lone floodlights spaced evenly across the ceiling. The only bright source of light came from the window of a small office at the far left corner of the wall closest to the front door. The door of the office opened rather slowly, and an older man stuck his head out of the door. Upon seeing Demi and Ronni, he sighed and said, "You two darn nearly gave me a heart attack." "Apologies, Reggie, my good man. We wanted to show a few friends the facility. You may carry on your business," Demi instructed, motioning for the security guard to return to his office. The guard waved a hand and turned back to the office, closing the door behind him. Demi turned his attention back to the trio. "Reggie is our night guard. He's a good fellow, likes the quiet around here. Also, he can barely hear, so he's an excellent choice of guard for our behind-closed-doors operations." Demi looked back at the security guard and waved to him. After the guard waved back, Demi held his hand to his head, extending his thumb and pinky and seeming to act out the motion of using a telephone. The guard's face quickly shifted into a look of grave concern, and he nodded and picked up the phone in his office. Demi turned back to the group, said, "A charming fellow indeed," and continued on. Becca and Benny shared a puzzled look.

As they walked through the facility, Benny still tried to

conceive of an escape plan. He'd never been in a situation where he'd needed to escape, but surely he could think of something that would help. There were piles of boxes all around the place, small drums of what he assume were chemicals and necessary fluids for machines, and various pieces of equipment and parts. Nothing really looked helpful, but maybe that was because he wasn't looking hard enough. There had to be something, a small detail or element he wasn't seeing. That was what the detectives looked for, right? Benny had to hold on to the belief that he could save the day. He didn't know how to be much of a hero, but he desperately wanted to be one for Becca's sake.

Demi and Ronni led them through the corridor of racks and boxes. Pallets full of boxes wrapped in plastic lined the aisles. Sometimes, the party had to squeeze through a row of pallets one at a time when the aisles were filled with shipments. In passing a shipment, Ronni bumped one of the pallets, and a small cloud of dust drifted toward Benny. His sneeze echoed across the high walls of the warehouse. "Do be careful, my friend," Demi sighed. "And apologies for the mess. Warehouse machinery often coats the air in an odd dust that is rather hard on the lungs, not to mention quite dirty to the touch." Benny, hearing this, looked at his hand resting on a metal runner. Lifting his hand, he saw a thin gray film coating his palm. The film appeared to also be on the wrapped pallets, leaving a gray glaze across the tightly bound plastic. Benny sneezed a second time, and Demi laughed. "Again: apologies, my friend. Sneeze again, and I'll begin to suspect that you're just looking for attention."

The party continued on through the warehouse, passing shipping and export packaging. Benny still hadn't thought of a plan, and he was beginning to worry that he never would. He rather wished that he could call for help or send a signal to someone. What he really needed was a way to call the police. He was just beginning to recall that he still had his cellphone when it began ringing. The party stopped moving, and Demi turned back to Benny. "Hmm, it appears you have someone requesting your attention." Demi strode to Benny and dug into his coat pocket, drawing the phone from Benny's coat and opening it. "Ah, it is Karen. I'm assuming she's a loved one?" Benny fumbled with an answer, awkwardly extending a glance to Becca despite his best effort to not do so, but Demi simply closed the phone. "I do detest interruptions, and I also do not like to share. She will have to wait." With that, he pocketed the phone into his own pants and continued onward. They walked three steps before the phone began ringing again. "Hmm, let's see who it is now. Ah, still Karen, desperate to reach you." He closed the phone a second time. "Come friends, let us make haste to-" and the phone rang again. "My my, you're quite the popular... oh, it's this Karen again. Gracious, madam, please take the hint." He closed the phone. They walked two steps, and the phone rang. This time, Demi turned the volume down on the phone until it was set to vibrate. "Now, no more interruptions," he said, and they continued walking. As they walked, no one said a word. The room was silent, all except for the almost constant buzzing coming from Demi's pocket. The buzz would stop for barely a few seconds before resuming. After a time, Demi stopped walking. "Sixteen. She has called you sixteen times. Sixteen times in," Demi said, checking his watch, "ten minutes. That is teetering on the brink of insanity." Benny sighed and said, "Yeah, she doesn't like Voicemail." Demi rolled his eyes and turned the phone off. "There, no more interruptions," he said, and they continued on their way. *Well, I can cross calling for help off my list of possible plans*, Benny thought.

"Ah, we have arrived," Demi declared as they reached a section of stacked boxes towards the back of the warehouse. In the middle of the pile sat a large box, much larger than the other boxes that were being shipped. Demi knelt down and patted the box. "This, my sweet, was all you had to do," Demi sighed. "You simply had to come to this box and remove the contents from the middle of the packing. It was that simple." He stood and walked over to Becca. She started to raise a hand to him, but her inner voice advised otherwise. Demi held his hand to her face and caressed her cheek. "I was so looking forward to our future together. This would have been more than enough to take us away from here. We could have been happy." Becca sneered and turned her head away from his hand. "I don't know what you're talking about, but there's no way in hell I'd ever go anywhere with you, you whack-job." Demi frowned and let go of his breath with a sigh. "You truly are a heart breaker. If I were you, I would have at least heard my offer before saying such crude, harsh things." Returning to his large box, Demi drew a small folding knife from his pocket and slit the tape on the top and sides. He looked up at his brother with a smile, saying, "Ronni, I suppose that means more for you and me." Ronni grinned with a smile like a crocodile and laughed, "Yes. Times will be good for us." "You don't even know the half of it, brother," Demi grinned. He reached into the box and slowly removed the pile of shirts in bags. Stacking them next to him, he finally reached the middle of the box.

With a bit of theatrical suspense, Demi removed the tightly bound white brick from the middle of the box while mimicking a cinematic theme. He stood and walked to his brother. "This, dear brother, will change everything." Ronni studied the folded white block in brown paper with a puzzled look. "Demi, is… is drugs?" Demi grinned and said, "No brother, this is not just 'drugs.' This is more than just a simple drug. This is cocaine, the purest I could get. This is going to change our lives. I already have buyers ready to move this product." He turned and looked to Becca. "This is what you gave up. You could have been a part of this empire, a ground floor contributor to a rising power in this dull, decrepit city. And yet you chose-" he paused, motioning to Benny, "this. Was it worth it?" Ronni reached out and held the bag. "I have never seen such many before." Demi smiled and put a hand on his brother's shoulder, saying, "Get used to it, Ronni. We are going to be big, so much bigger than we have ever dreamed."

Benny didn't know a lot about drugs, but that was mostly because there hadn't been any drug-related crimes to speak of in the city. Any crimes that had occurred were only considered drug-related because the persons involved were high at the time. He had to assume that drug trafficking wasn't happening, as the news hadn't reported any such events. If Demi and Ronni did indeed sell this cocaine in the city, they would certainly be opening up the drug trade business in the city. With no competition, they could easily become kingpins. At least, that's what Benny assumed would happen. He didn't really have any idea how the drug trade worked, but he'd seen enough in the crime shows to know that kingpins were formed and the industry could rise from just two thugs looking to start selling. That had to at least be vaguely true to life.

Demi and Ronni looked over their product for a moment more before Demi turned his attention back to Becca. He walked over to her and stood just a bit too close, staring into her eyes. She grimaced and, through gritted teeth, said, "Okay, you have your shit. Now let us go." Demi shook his head and gestured vaguely to the items around them. "No, my love, I cannot do that. You see, this doesn't look good for us. Someone will know what we've done here tonight. We need to be certain that there are no loose ends in this matter, and that is why I've made an executive decision." Demi smiled and raised a hand to her face, grazing her cheek with his fingers. "I need you, one last time, to help me. I need you to-" but Becca cut him off, slapping his hand away and screaming, "You don't get it! I won't help you! Ever!" Demi sighed and turned his back on her, rubbing his forehead. Stepping a little to the right, he threw a hand in the air and waved broadly toward the guard's office. "You don't really have a say in the matter. You see I really do need you for this. I have to have you take the blame. This calls for a new fall guy, or in this case, a fall girl."

Before Demi could explain further, the security guard came out of his office. He walked around the corner of the racks and stood, looking somewhat odd, as if he were nervous. "Somethin' I can do for you, Mr. Tzetki? I'm trying to watch "Copper Badge." Benny smiled and said, "Oh, that's my favorite show. Which episode is it?" Demi did not smile. Instead, Demi drew a pistol from his waistband and fired twice upon the guard, shooting him in the chest and arm. The guard cried out in a gasp of pain and surprise, falling to the floor. He kicked three times in a kind of panicked convulsion and then lay still. Becca gasped and Benny screamed in a rather high voice. Demi held the pistol by his side. Turning his attention to Becca, he spoke in a far quieter voice: "As I was saying, I need you to take the fall for this. I cannot have loose ends. I do have an image to maintain." Benny looked at the poor guard lying lifeless on the floor and knew that time was running out. He needed to get a grip on the situation. If he didn't act soon, Becca could be the next victim on the floor.

"This wasn't supposed to be the plan, you see," Demi continued, pacing and swinging the pistol by his side. "Initially, I preferred the plan we discussed. You were to choose a male subject that would serve as an appropriate mark, lead him here and have him assist you in the 'robbery' as it were, and finally leave him here at the scene to be discovered by the police. That seemed to be the best solution to my problem." Demi stopped pacing and turned his attention to Becca. "The problem came about when your loyalty was called into question. And yes, though I do approve of your choice of mark, I believe that you have not taken this firm's best interest to heart when making your choices. I believe that you might actually care for this man," he said, waving the gun at Benny. "He isn't the mark. He was never meant to be the mark. I kept trying to tell you that. He isn't a part of this," Becca said, stamping her foot in frustration. Benny furrowed his brow and said, "I'm sorry, but I'm not familiar with this. What exactly is a mark, and why am I not one?" Demi laughed and replied, "My friend, a 'mark,' as we like to call them, is a person that is chosen to be used in a con or operation. For example, in this case, Ms. Becca has chosen you to be the mark for this heist. You were to be led here by our lovely thief, brought to this spot before the aforementioned box, and then shot and left here for the authorities to find and arrest. You were meant to 'take the fall.'"

Benny turned to Becca, looking into her eyes. He looked for any sign of truth in Demi's explanation. She was talking to him, saying things that probably sounded like "It's not true," but he could see in her face that it definitely was. He began to replay the evening in his mind. He remembered all of the moments that he shared with her, and he began to see the times that she had known. He could see her standing in the park, looking across the street. He could see her there in the street outside Lee's, looking at the van in which he would later be held prisoner. There were many times that she had clearly been working, in some form or other, with this group. But, then he thought about the park. He thought about the moment beneath his tree, the moment when she had left him. She looked so sad for him, and he could see it there on her face. He saw that now, the look of regret and shame on her face, and he knew.

"You were never supposed to be here," Becca was saying, tears beginning to come to her eyes. Benny grinned and said, "It's okay. I believe you. Don't worry about me." Becca's face relaxed, and she began to smile. Demi gritted his teeth and shouted, "Stop that! Stop that right now. Do not comfort her. She is not yours to be consoled. You are not hers. You are nothing to her." With a sharp gasp of breath, Demi screamed, "You cannot have what is mine!" The room echoed with his exclamation. Even Ronni seemed shaken by this outburst. Clearing his throat and wiping his brow, Demi gathered himself and said, "Sadly, it seems I cannot have her either. She has chosen a path that does not follow my own. I knew this to be true when we were standing at the embankment, looking down on this very place. So, with no other option left, my wonderful cunning provided a new plan, and I must say that this one is much better."

Demi turned to the open box and moved it a little to the right. "Ronni," he said to his statuesque brother, "be a dear and hold our friends for a moment. I need to set this scene properly." Ronni looked at his brother with a furrowed brow. "You want I hold them in place?" "Yes, my good man," Demi replied, walking over to the body of the security guard. As Ronni grasped both Becca and Benny in his enormous hands, Demi walked over to the body of the recently employed/living Reggie and pulled the guard's pistol from the holster. Returning to his makeshift crime scene, he looked at the two captives, stuck his own pistol behind his back in his belt, and rubbed his chin. "Hmm, move her a little to the left. Yes, that's it." Ronni did as instructed, shoving Becca to the side. "Now move him a little forward." Ronni led Benny forward a few steps. "Ah," Demi said, "That's perfect." He raised his hand to Ronni with a beckoning motion. "I let go now?" Ronni asked. Demi nodded, and Ronni joined him on the other side.

"Being a good improviser has many advantages," Demi said, grinning. "One of those is that you always find a way out. And so I began to think, 'What ever shall I do if Ms. Becca does not wish to help us in our efforts?' It was then that I came to terms with the sad state of affairs: Ms. Becca and I must say 'Adieu' and bid our romance a fond farewell." Demi studied the gun he had taken from the guard's holster. "I decided that this would look much better if Ms. Becca were left at the scene with her mark. I have already taken the liberty of contacting the police and telling them that two questionable subjects have broken into the warehouse, vis a vi the services of our dearly departed Reggie," he said with a delicate tone, and Ronni performed a sluggish Sign Of The Cross over his barrel chest. "When the authorities do arrive, which they should any moment, they will find an expert thief and her henchman robbing a prominent business and murdering said guard. Thus, you must be the new mark, as it were, and I am sad to be the bearer of such bad news. My dear, it has been a joy and a delight, but I do believe this means we are breaking up." With that, Demi raised the guard's pistol and fired on Becca, striking her in the shoulder. She howled in pain and felt backwards onto the floor.

Benny gasped in panic, shouting some kind of mixed growl and scream. He dropped to her side, almost catching her before she hit the ground. "Oh God, oh God, are you okay?" he said, begging for more information about her condition. She groaned in pain and grasped his hand, squeezing it like a stress ball. "I'm okay, it's just in the muscle." Benny didn't know what to do, but he'd heard that victims of gunshots typically began to chill as their bodies tried to fight the pain and infection from the bullet wound. Benny unfastened his jacket and threw it over Becca's shoulders, pulling it around her. "You don't... I'm not... just wait," Becca said, but she could barely focus from the pain. Benny pulled the jacket down to her side and closed it around her torso. As he did, he felt a heavy lump in the pocket. Suddenly, he remembered exactly what was in that pocket. Reaching in while covering the action with his body, he drew out the pistol. Holding it tightly, he looked in Becca's eyes and, not knowing anything else to do, winked.

Demi scoffed at the two on the floor. "Oh for God's sake. It's just a flesh wound. She'll be fine. I do have to make it look as if our security staff was performing in the line of duty," he said, chuckling in some kind of sick delight. He gently tossed the gun down by the guard's lifeless body. Benny looked over his shoulder and saw his opportunity. He stood and raised his pistol, pointing it square at Demi's chest. Demi laughed as he turned his attention back to Benny, but he stopped the moment he saw the firearm.

"Oh my," Demi sighed, "You seem to have gotten the better of me." "Damn right I did," Benny said, enjoying how cool it sounded echoing off the walls of the warehouse. "Drop your gun." Demi stood still, studying Benny's face. Then, his eyes moved to the gun itself. Benny grew impatient. "I said, 'Drop it.' Do it now." Demi kept his eyes on the pistol in Benny's hand. Finally, a small grin grew on his face. Reaching into his belt, he drew out his pistol and tossed it to the ground far from his feet. He held a hand out before him. "Oh please, kind sir. Do not shoot," he said, chuckling to himself.

Benny's face was growing hot with anger. He knew that shooting Demi wasn't the right thing to do, especially with the police coming, but he couldn't think of anything that he wanted more right now. Demi was a monster, and he wanted so very badly to punish him. Ronni started toward his brother, but Demi held his hand to stop him. "No, my brother, this is between us two." "What? Do you have plan? Stop him," Ronni begged, but Demi simply grinned and crossed his arms defiantly. Benny tried to remain calm and rational, but that smug grin of Demi's only made his anger worse. "I do not believe you want to do this, friend," Demi teased. "No, right now I want nothing more than this," Benny said, a devilish grin creeping over his face.

Becca stared up from the floor, a look of both shock and pain draped over her face. Ronni growled beside his brother but remained motionless. Demi sighed and laughed. He said with a chuckle, "You do not have the kind of fortitude that it takes to-" but Benny cut him off, saying, "Oh just shut up," and pulled the trigger.

CHAPTER TWELVE

Benny could feel the heat of his anger on his face. Only a moment before, he had doubted his resolve to shoot Demi, but that moment was now defeated by his hatred for the man. He was proud of himself for having the guts to pull the trigger. It was then that Benny began to assess the situation before him. The gun had not gone off. Benny looked down to the pistol. He had left the safety on. Before he could switch the safety off, Demi was on him, ripping the gun from his hands and turning it on him. "If you're going to shoot someone, know how the damn gun works beforehand, my friend," Demi sneered.

Benny held his hands up in surrender. "Oh don't do that," Demi frowned. "It makes you look like a silly bandit in some childish western film." "Oh, uh, sorry," Benny mumbled, putting his hands down. "That's better," Demi said, smiling. "Take it like a man. You know, there is a kind of poetry in being shot with your own handgun. I hope you do relish in the beauty of it." As Demi moved his finger inside the trigger guard, Becca reached up from the floor and took Benny's hand. "Thank you for standing up for me," Becca said, trying her best to smile. Demi shouted, "No, unhand him. He is not protecting you. He has put you in further danger." "He didn't shoot me. You did," she replied.

Demi ran his fingers through his hair as a groan came roaring up from his gut. He stomped his foot against the pallet lying next to him, shaking the gun in frustration. "Is this really how you wanted things? You had all the power here. You could have simply accepted my generous offer and performed amicably. You chose this." "Like hell I did," Becca said, groaning from the pain. "I told you I was finished. You just can't let go. Everything has to be yours. You're an idiot child who's mad that he can't have his toys." "A child, am I?" Demi scoffed, his teeth clenched like a feral beast. "Well maybe my toys are broken. Perhaps I simply don't need to play with them any longer." Demi jerked the gun up toward Benny's head. Benny knew with one look at his eyes that Demi wanted to and would kill him. Granted, the gun pointed at his head was a pretty good indicator, but still.

Ronni put his hand on Demi's shoulder. "Brother, do you not think that kill him is bad? We need him live, yes?" Demi paused, grinding his teeth. His eyes were quivering with rage, but they soon began to settle, and he seemed to collect his fiery hate within himself. "You make a fine point," Demi said, "But I think we can have one casualty today and still accomplish our goals. The police would probably simply consider it a double-cross and carry on, especially when they find Miss Becca's fingerprints on this gun." Ronni cocked his head to the side for a moment, as if this thought had to run its course through his brain, and then laughed. "You are clever, brother. Is good plan." Benny looked down at Becca, who was still struggling to even breathe, and returned his gaze to Demi. He tried his best to mask the fear in his voice. "What are you going to do? Are you going to just kill me and hope that the police assume she did it? That sounds like a rough plan to me." Benny wondered if now was the best time to critique Demi's abilities as a criminal mastermind, but it wasn't like Benny had many other options for diversion.

Demi kept the gun at eye line with Benny. "You do not matter, and you are no concern in this operation. You were a simple lackey and nothing more. Sadly, you have become something more troublesome. Miss Becca seems to think highly of you." He turned, looking into Becca's eyes. Becca's face seemed to be turning white. She looked at Demi, then at Benny, and then looked back at Demi. "I would even go so far as to say she might deeply care for you. Look at her face. You can see the light for you in her eyes." He had been grinning, but his grin turned to a sneer. "That will not do. There is not enough room in her life for more than one man, and I certainly do not like to share. Therefore," he turned his attention to Benny again, "I think it's time for you to die."

Demi cocked the hammer back on the pistol, and Benny felt his heart stop. He knew that Demi was going to kill him. For all his trying and wishing for some kind of answer or release from his misery, Benny would finally get his wish. And in that moment, staring down the barrel of a lunatic, he begged God, the universe, Buddha, and anyone else that might be listening to let him live. He wanted a chance to change his life, to live and believe in himself, to see the world as a conquest that he could tame and overpower. He had absolutely no idea what he would do if given the chance to live, but, God in heaven, did he ever want that chance.

The next few moments were a blur. As Demi's finger closed on the trigger, Benny had just enough clarity of mind to notice a small wad of beige and brown sticking out of the gun's barrel. He did not, however, have enough time to think more on this before the gun exploded. The barrel had been clogged with mulch and dirt from Benny's earlier visit to his favorite tree, causing the round to explode in the chamber. The smoke and blast from the gun immediate shook both Demi and Ronni, causing Demi to throw the gun in sudden alarm. Benny, stunned by the realization that he was not going to die, screamed in shock and joy. He turned to help Becca off the floor, but she was already on her feet, grasping his arm and saying, "Run, you idiot!"

Benny shook his haze of delight, and the two dashed into the field of boxes and racks. Benny tried his best to protect Becca, shielding her with his body in case Demi tried to shoot again with his own gun, but she was quickly out running him. She looked back over her wounded shoulder at him and whispered, "You need to hide. Now." "But I can't just leave you alone. He'll kill you," Benny said. She grabbed him, hearing Demi cry out in anger while cocking his pistol, and pulled them low behind a stack of boxes. "No, no he won't. I know him, and I know how he feels about me. He's angry, and he has a hell of a temper, but he will never hurt me." Benny looked at her shoulder, and she took notice, saying, "Okay, yeah, he'll hurt me, but he won't kill me." "Is your shoulder okay? How much are you bleeding?" Benny begged, reaching out to her shoulder. As he lifted the jacket, she laughed, "Bleeding? Jeeze, they were rubber bullets. Reggie was a terrible guard, always worried he'd kill someone, so he only ever carried rubber bullets. Thank God that Demi doesn't know that." Benny drew the jacket back along with her running jacket to reveal her highly bruised shoulder. "Yeesh," Benny said with a grimace, "You might not be bleeding, but you're gonna feel that later, assuming we see a later."

From the end of the aisles, Demi and Ronni were calling to each other, shouting commands in their native language. "You have to move fast," Becca commanded. "You need to get out of here. I'll be fine. Just go." Benny frowned and said, "No way. I'm not leaving you. I can take them." Becca stared at him. "Really? You can? You can take them both? Well them, macho man, show me your moves. You'll totally live through that. You should probably use Kung Fu, right?" Benny looked back at the aisles, hearing the heavy footsteps of the two men and said, "Okay, perhaps I should go with hiding." Before they could say another word, the voice of Demi called out from the aisle beside them: "Come now, dear friends. This simply will not do. You're only making this matter worse for yourselves."

Becca turned her head back to Benny to tell him to run for the door, but he was gone. She looked about herself but saw nothing. Suddenly, a small chunk of wood fell on her shoulder, striking her near the wound. She cupped her hand over her mouth, muffling the cry of pain, and looked up. Benny was scaling the side of the rack, albeit in a rather awkward manner. He looked down at her and whispered, "Oh crap, sorry," but she waved her hand wildly at him, indicating he should continue his climb. Benny turned his attention back to the boxes and pallets before him. In no time, he had reached the summit of the rack. Scrambling to gather himself atop the high rise, he tried his best to not look down. He did not try very hard, and he really wished he had.

Demi turned the corner and found Becca slumped against a loaded pallet. "Ah, so here you are. I was beginning to worry you'd left me, but I see that he left you," Demi chuckled. "Yep, he's a jerk. Just took off. I bet he's long gone by now. No sense in looking for him," Becca groaned, but Demi jerked her up off the floor by her bad arm. "You and I both know he's here somewhere. When we find him, I'm certain he'll see our side of things. Ronni can prove quite convincing, especially with his hands on..." but Becca stopped him. "Yeah, I get it. Ronni's gonna beat him up. God, shut up already." Demi scoffed, "Spoilsport," and led her around the aisle. From high above, Benny watched as Demi shoved Becca over toward the center of the warehouse. He slouched against the stacked boxes and tried to remain unseen. Demi pushed Becca to the floor and called out to his brother. "Ronni, dear, do be a good lad and find him, post haste. We are a bit pressed for time."

Benny moved to the top of the rack and tried his best to slink along the tops of the boxes. As he moved, he tried to be certain that he wouldn't make any noticeable noise, but the plastic wrap around the boxes coupled with the soft crunch of his weight on cardboard made that rather challenging. He was just about to reach the edge of the rack to get a better view of Demi and Becca when he heard Ronni calling out below: "Do not worry, brother. I find him soon. He is little mouse, trying to escape maze." Benny knew that he'd never get the drop on Demi without first doing something about Ronni. Turning back from the edge, he focused his attention on the floor beneath him. Benny had never really had a problem with heights, but he had to admit that this was far more terrifying than he'd expected. Easing his way down between two loaded pallets of boxes, he edged his way toward the lip of the rack.

He knew that he had to move to the next rack. He couldn't

remain there for long. Surely Ronni would look there soon. *Maybe I can jump across.* He tried to tell himself that the gap between the racks wasn't nearly as long as it seemed, but he knew that wasn't true. The racks were easily eight feet apart, and he wasn't sure of his athleticism, but he had a pretty good hunch that leaping wasn't his strong suit. *I need a ladder or something, some way to get across without touching the ground.* He looked about himself, but he couldn't find a board or anything that might bridge the gap. There was no way around it. If he were going to get across, he'd have to jump.

Studying the upper level of the rack, he saw a shorter pallet that had far less of a load. The boxes were partially stacked, as if workers had pulled some from that pallet load. *Maybe I can jump into that pocket and catch my fall on the boxes.* Carefully positioning his feet, he sidled against the pallets of the rack, inching closer to his target. *This is easily the stupidest thing I've ever thought of. There is no way I'm going to make this jump.* He started to climb back up, but then he thought about Ronni's hands crushing his windpipe. This was, though hard to believe, a better option than giving up. Easing himself against the pallet's edge, he readied himself for the jump. He knew that there would be no soft, easy landing. He also knew he'd have to hustle once he landed. Ronni would hear this without a doubt, and he'd need to hide quickly. With any luck, he might be able to use the same boxes to climb up to the top.

Is there any way I'm supposed to prepare myself for this? Benny decided the best course would be to jump without thinking about it any further. With a quick turn, he lunged forward from the boxes, vaulting across the gap toward the short pallet stack. He surprised himself at how far he actually traveled, but that surprise quickly turned to anguish. He had not considered how thick and solid boxes full of t-shirts would actually be. The impact took the wind out of his lungs as he landed hard against the solid boxes. He hoped that he hadn't let out as loud a groan as it seemed, but he heard Ronni quickly stepping toward the sound. Scrambling, he barely reached the top of the rack before Ronni rounded the corner. "Brother," Ronni called out, "I think he is maybe monkey." Demi laughed and said, "I don't really know what you meant by that, but I trust your better judgment." Benny fell back against the boxes, trying to gather himself. He was still gasping for air, but his wits were returning to him. *Okay, no more jumping if I can help it.*

Looking about him, he saw that a few of the racks were connected by higher aisle hangs. Most of them did not have pallets, but they did have wire grates laid over the runners, presumably to allow for extra pallet storage at the highest reaches *I could probably use those to get around much easier.* Benny didn't fancy himself a high-wire acrobat, but he'd surprised himself enough today to be game for anything. Easing over to the edge of one of the runners, he crouched down just in case Ronni might be nearby. As he did, he ran his hand over the edge of the steel support. The support was cold like most of the metal in the building, but this felt different than the rest. He pulled his hand away and looked at his palm. That same fine film of dust had gathered on his hand. *This stuff is disgusting. It's all over everything in this place.* Benny started to rub his pant leg with his hand, but he decided he didn't want the dirt on his clothes any more than it already was. He wiped his hand on a nearby box. He stopped and studied the side of the box. *Good grief, this stuff is so think it leaves a hand print. I can't imagine working-* Benny cut his thought short as an idea began to work its way to the front of his mind.

Becca lay on the ground at Demi's feet. Her shoulder still stung from the blow, but she was coming to terms with the pain. She had tried her best to learn to manage pain, knowing that she'd injure herself many times while thieving. This, however, was quite a rare pain, one for which she'd never prepared. She needed a way to help Benny, but she couldn't think of much that she could do, especially considering her armed guard. Demi wouldn't kill her, but he could very well shoot her, and she was certain that his ammunition wasn't made of rubber. *I have to do something. I have to help Ben,* Becca thought, looking around her for something or some way to distract Demi. *Well, at least I can get him talking.*

"You know," she began, trying her best to sound like she wasn't in pain, "If you're trying to win my heart and keep my company, this isn't the best way to do it. I gotta say, you're not coming off as terribly attractive here." Demi laughed, still keeping his eyes on the action across the way, and said, "Well drat. I do suppose I should have at least done something with my hair." "You could also stand to lose a few or twenty pounds," Becca said, knowing his physique was a major pressure point. "Oh, now you're just being coarse," he scoffed, but she knew very well she'd poked the right button. Demi loved to proclaim himself a mastermind and a confident, strong leader, but the truth was that he suffered from a weak ego. Granted, he had plenty of qualities that helped to boost that ego, but they were all shallow elements that barely did more than carry him from moment to moment. His fitness was probably the greatest of these weaknesses, and she knew this well. In fact, one of the major reasons that she'd begun working out recently was because he often told her to maintain a level of fit. She had secretly hoped that he'd see her later in her progress and regret losing her. This, however, was not what she had intended.

Using a metal table next to her for support, she stood, trying her best to not use her bad arm. "No, I'm serious. You really do look a bit worse for the wear. It seems like you've just let yourself go." He turned his attention to her, and she knew she'd gotten to him. "How dare you say such things to me? You have never once complained about my appearance, let alone the caliber of my body. As I recall," he said, stepping toward her, "there was a time when you were quite the fan of my build." *Good meat head. That's a good meat head.* "I mean, I guess it's pretty good. I just feel like time hasn't been very good to you this past month. Have you been snacking more? It sure seems like it." She could see in his face that he was preoccupied now, and if she could keep him this way, he would surely drop his guard and maybe even the gun soon. "Madam, I will have you know that I maintain a less-than-fifteen-percent body fat composition at all times, and you of all people should know this. If anything, time away from you has hardened my focus on my physical stature," he said with a slight growl in his voice. *Now I'm really getting to him. Keep it up, girl. Catch him when he's down.*

Becca turned on the sassy smirk she had perfected, having used it many times before on many men, this particular man included. "Eh, I'm just not seeing it." Demi raised his eyebrows and laughed. "Not seeing it? Do you jest? Look at this chest!" He yanked his shirt up, revealing his stacked abs and chiseled muscle lines. He definitely hadn't gained a single pound, and there was certainly a time where she'd been immediately aroused by the sight of his toned chest, but now she saw something else in those muscles: the focus of a man that didn't care for her like he cared for himself. Trying her best to not show her disdain, she replied with a chuckle, "No, see, right there. Right above the hip line. That's fat right there. You've gained some right there, and that's just the first spot I see." "This is absurd," he barked, placing the gun down on the table next to him. "I am in the height of my perfection. Observe." With that, he dropped to the ground in one fluid motion and began performing one-handed push-ups.

This was her chance. His guard was down, and he wasn't thinking clearly. All she had to do was rush to the table's edge and grab the gun. Maybe she could even kick him while he was down and disorient him. *Gotta act fast here. If he gets the upper hand on you, you'll never beat him.* Rolling her body weight onto the balls of her feet, she primed herself to strike.

Just as she tensed her muscles to dash to the table, Demi sprung from the floor, slamming his hand down upon the table and on top of the pistol. His grin was almost clownishly enormous, and she felt her stomach immediately knot itself three times over. "Oh you are absurd. You're a gem, a true delight. Did you honestly think you had distracted me from the situation at hand?" Becca attempted to form words, but the air in her voice fell over dry vocal cords. She tried her best to seem calm, but she knew she was failing. "I honestly cannot fathom how you think so little of me as to assume that I'd be disarmed over something so petty. Do I look like some kind of simpleton to you? This is honestly rather pathetic, especially coming from you. Have I not taught you better than this?"

She finally found her voice and tried her best to test his nerve. "Well, go ahead. Shoot me. You know you want to." He smirked and eyed her with almost a look of pity. "Oh, that's precious. I had hoped you would be stronger than to further test my resolve, but I see now that you think you can control me. No, I do not wish to shoot you," he said, lifting the gun from the table and removing the magazine. After locking the slide back and setting the pistol down, he smiled and said, "No, shooting you seems archaic now, like putting down a wounded horse or a bad dog. I think you deserve a more civilized method." He stepped toward her, and she felt panic rising behind her eyes. "Think of it as fair punishment. You've broken my heart, so I shall break several of your bones. And goodness knows I like putting my hands on you," he said, raising his large, powerful hands toward her. She looked in his eyes, saw the truth of his words and intent, and ran. The sound of his footsteps behind her thundered across the walls.

Elsewhere, Benny was still trying to elude Ronni. The big lug had taken to throwing his weight around on piles of boxes, attempting to scare Benny from behind every stack. Occasionally, he would also throw himself up to the second level of the racks, proceeding to do the same thing with boxes there. The man was absurdly strong and quite agile, two qualities that Benny did not possess. Just seeing him climb the rack runners made Benny sick. *The guy's a powerhouse, and I am in big trouble. This is, by far, the craziest thing I've ever thought of doing.* Moving as quickly as he could, Benny worked his way over to a section of white shipping boxes in the middle of the aisle. Thankfully, these rows were connected with runners above, keeping him from having to leap again. As quietly as he could, he leaned down and printed his dust-covered hand on a nearby box across from the hanging rod. Scrambling back into place as quickly as possible, he waited until Ronni came his direction. Ronni looked up from his search and saw the hand print. "Heh heh," he laughed with a kind of growl in his voice. "Where are you, friend? Do not make hard for yourself." *This is it. I have to act now.*

Benny moved to the edge of the runners by his platform. *This is absolutely crazy. What the hell am I doing?* Ronni was leaning between aisles, looking for him. "Come out now," he called. "I make quick for you. No pain. Is best." He looked down the nearby aisle and then turned his back on Benny's position. Before he could convince himself that this plan was insane, Benny leaped from the runner. He flew through the air, grasping the rod that held the hanging shirts. He was no gymnast, but he did have a decent grip. As he swung upward from the jump, he thrust his heels into the back of Ronni's head. Ronni barked from the pain of the impact and staggered forward, ramming his head into the upright of the riser nearby. The sound was excruciating just to hear. Ronni stumbled for a moment, and then fell to the floor. His eyes wandered for a moment, but they soon closed. Benny looked down from his hanging position above the huge thug. *I think he's out cold. Of course, he might also be dead. Man, I hope I didn't just kill him.*

Becca was running out of things to either hide behind or knock in front of Demi as she ran. Vaulting over an assembly line, she stopped short, throwing boxes and anything else she could grab at him. "This is absurd," Demi shouted, using his arms to block his body and face from the onslaught of projectiles. "You should simply give up and let me break your arms." She laughed and said, "I'd like to see you try," but the truth was that she did not want to even give him the chance. She knew very well that he could and would do so, and that fear was beginning to get to her. *I need the upper hand on him. I can fight him, but only if I get a few unguarded blows in.*

Demi had, very early in their relationship, taught her a few hand-to-hand combat techniques, mostly street brawler mechanics, but he'd stopped rather abruptly when she began beating him in their sparring matches. His size and strength were unmatched, but she could attack so much faster than him, and her agility was something with which he just couldn't compete. Without his knowing, she had continued her practice, picking up small lessons and skills online. Granted, losing her hulking sparring partner made lessons a little harder to master, but she had been proud of the extra credit learning she'd acquired. The question was if she could put that learning to use.

Grasping a rolled tube of packing material, she slung it at his head. He caught it, yanking it away from her hold. The tube, blocking his eyesight, gave him no warning as she swept beneath the assembly rollers and took his legs out. He fell with an ungodly thud despite his best efforts to catch himself on the rollers. Becca used the time to get to her feet, running back toward the table where the gun still lay. She had almost reached the table when the tube struck her in the back, knocking her to the ground. Before she could recover, he was on her, lunging at her and pinning her to the ground. His weight was more than she could have expected, but she still found a moment to thrust a knee into his side. The strike lessened his grip just enough for her work an arm loose. Grabbing the tube, she rammed the edge of it into the side of his head, knocking him to the side in a daze.

She had just made her way to her feet and was returning to the table when he grabbed her leg, gripping her ankle like a shackle. She pulled against his grip, feeling like her leg might come out of socket. "Let me go, you psychopath," she barked. "Oh, my," he scoffed. "Well, as you insist." With that, he let her leg go, giving a shove against her extended foot. The push sent her crashing into the table, sending the gun and magazine sliding across the floor. The table overturned, landing her on a pile of shipping boxes. As she pulled herself from the rubble and stood, she searched the floor for the gun. Finally, her eyes fell on the gun, but it was unfortunately in Demi's outstretched hand. "This ends now," he said, gritting his teeth.

"What? Are you gonna shoot me? You gonna kill me?" Becca asked this with sarcasm painted over her words, but that was merely there to mask the fear. She knew very well he might now. "Please understand that you drove me to this, dearest. Your incessant complications have sullied my intent, and I do not see a way out of this," he replied, having exchanged his gritted teeth for a growing smile. "You really should have taken my offer. We could have been happy together." "Your offer? Are you seriously still making this about us?" Suddenly, a bit of the fear subsided in her. An anger was brewing deep in her gut. "This is why I couldn't be with you. You were always doing something reckless and arrogant, always putting your stupid plan before us. Everything has and always will be about you. There was never any room in your life for me. There never will be."

As if they were trading anger and hatred, Demi seemed to take on a bit of hers and turn the heat up.

"You harlot witch. I've done everything I possibly can for you. I gave you anything you asked for. I made you what you are, what you wanted to be."

"No," Becca growled, "You made me something else. You may have given me the jobs, but I never asked to be a part of this mess. You put me here because you need me. You used me."

"I? I need you? Is that so? Were it not for me, you'd still be trying to pick pockets in the park. Without me, you'd be working some diner as a waitress. You talk as if you had a future before me, or do you so easily forget how pathetic you were before I pulled you from your worthless abyss?"

"My life is not better because of you. If you gave me anything, it's nothing but a lifetime of regret. I've hurt a lot of people, and I don't want that misery anymore. But go ahead. Tell me all the ways I'd be miserable without you. Enlighten me, genius. Take all the time you need."

Demi opened his mouth to speak, but the words never came. He stopped, furrowed his brow, and then smiled.

"Oh, that's precious. You think you can keep me talking."

Shit.

"That's it exactly, isn't it? You're adorable. You think I'll just stand here arguing with you until the police arrive. You think you can distract me."

Think, Becca, think. Damn it, you're in trouble.

"You know, I once considered you a treasure, a jewel I had stolen from the world. Perhaps I was never so open and honest about my feelings, but then again, perhaps that means you and I were never meant to be."

This is it. He's going to do it. Oh, God.

Demi tightened his grip on the pistol, extending his arm fully toward her head.

"I think it's time we say, 'Adieu.' I shall miss you dearly, my love. I'll especially miss that wonderful body of yours."

Becca felt warm tears coming to her eyes. She was honestly surprised by the amount of panic welling up in her chest. "Go to hell, you son of a bitch," She snarled. "You first, dear," he replied. Becca braced herself for the pain, knowing she wouldn't feel it for long. And then, she heard a whirring, like some kind of small motor. And it was getting louder.

CHAPTER THIRTEEN

Benny had never hit anyone with a golf cart before. To be fair though, he had never really driven a golf cart with any intent of hitting someone. This day seemed to be full of firsts for him. He had tried to think of a better plan, but the golf cart idea was the best he could generate. Once he'd gotten down from the hanging rod, a feat that began as an elegant jump and turned into a haphazard fall, he began scrambling, looking for something to incapacitate Demi. As he darted across the floor of the warehouse, he saw nothing but boxes and pallets. Occasionally he'd find a hand tool of some kind, but these were always too small for any real stopping power. He scrambled through the place, trying to find something big, something that he could use to strike a hard blow. And then he found the golf cart.

The golf cart was parked near the far wall of the warehouse. Benny grinned and ran to the cart. He found the battery cable and unplugged it, making sure he didn't make too much noise. He couldn't be certain, but he thought he heard Becca and Demi arguing. *I hope she has him distracted. There's no way he won't hear me coming.* He jumped into the driver's seat of the golf cart and turned the key. The cart sounded a soft beep, and a small green light began glowing on the dash. Benny looked around for any other things he needed to disconnect on the cart. Satisfied, he pressed down on the gas pedal, and the cart leaped forward, crashing into a few nearby boxes. Something on the roof of the cart began knocking around. *Okay, easy buddy. You can do this. Don't rush.* Slowly, Benny backed the cart up and pulled out of the makeshift parking space. He moved the golf cart over to the aisle that lined up almost perfectly with Demi. Benny took a slow breath. *You get one chance at this. Don't waste it.* With that thought, he slammed on the gas pedal.

Demi was pointing the pistol right at Becca when Benny hit him. The golf cart was barely pushing fifteen miles per hour, but the impact was enough to knock Demi to the floor, slamming his head against the metal edge of the assembly line nearby. His cry of pain echoed across the walls and sounded like the roar of a great beast being taken down in the hunt. The golf cart slammed to a stop upon impact, and Benny rocked forward in the seat, banging his head against the top rail of the cabin. Unbeknown to Benny, a bucket of industrial liquid adhesive was sitting on the top of the cart's cabin. The bucket tumbled forward, breaking the lid and spilling the contents all over Demi. He laid on the ground, gently groaning, yet unable to gather himself. He seemed to be knocked out. "Holy crap," Becca said, her eyes wide with surprise. "Oh God I think I killed him too," Benny said, fumbling out of the seat. He staggered over to Demi's side and looked down at his fallen foe, but he quickly shook the concern from his mind. Demi clearly wasn't dead, and Benny clearly didn't care. He reached into Demi's pocket and grabbed his cell phone, shaking off some of the liquid adhesive.

"Are you okay?" he asked, rushing to Becca's side. She looked down at Demi, looked at the mess, and then back at Benny. "You... you beat them both? How did... what did... you're amazing," she finally uttered, still somewhat out of breath from the shock. The two of them stood, staring into each other's eyes, until Becca gasped and remembered. "Oh crap, the police are coming. We gotta get out of here." Benny's eyes widened with the realization of this news, and the two dashed for the door of the warehouse. Benny suddenly stopped and said, "The evidence!" Turning around, he dashed back to the remains of his pistol, pocketed the damaged gun, and dashed back toward the door.

Outside, the quiet barely even showed signs of the struggle inside the warehouse. Benny and Becca flung the door open and raced out into the barely lit dirt grounds. "We gotta hide, or run, or something," Becca said, hearing the sirens far off in the distance. The two dashed up the embankment and began running down the road. The highway was relatively lit by the moon, so their vision wasn't completely impaired. Still, they definitely saw the lights of the squad cars coming well before they arrived. Becca turned to Benny and looked over his shoulder at the ditch beside them. "Get over here." Benny barely had time to respond before she grabbed his jacket and pulled him off the road. The two tumbled into the ditch beside the road with Becca on top of Benny. "Don't move," Becca said, her eyes looking away as she listened for the sirens. The squad cars came by the road and passed, but one car stopped near their spot. "Damn it," Becca muttered. The spot from the car came alive with light, and the officer stepped out of his car, pointing the light towards the ditch. "He's spotted us. Don't move," Becca said, shooting Benny a look. As the light traced the ditch and quickly approached them, Becca's eyes grew wide and she grasped Benny's head, locking him in a passionate kiss. Instinctively, Benny threw his arms around her back and held her close. The light hit them, but Becca did not break the kiss. "Okay, love birds," the officer called out. "Time to move along." Becca broke the kiss and looked back at the policeman. "Okay, okay, sheesh. We're going. Kill the romance, why don't ya," she groaned, helping Benny stand. The officer turned off his spot and got back in his car, speeding off to rejoin the group. Becca dusted herself off, but Benny stood there. "Um... good plan," Benny finally said. Becca looked at him, grinned, and said, "Yeah, very good plan." Benny grew red and began dusting himself to hide his face.

The two walked down the road for a long time, neither saying a word. The highway ran almost straight into the city, but they still had a few miles to walk. During their walk, they kept their eyes mostly forward. The two seemed to be locked in some kind of trance, each reflecting on the evening. As they neared the city, their spirits seemed to grow lighter and brighter with the approaching glow of the lights. At one point, Benny had a moment of clear thought and wondered if he should hold Becca's hand, but he couldn't think of a single thing to say or do to introduce that, so the thought diminished in his mind. Soon, they had reached Union Street. They gathered next to a group of pedestrians at the corner, all waiting on the crossing sign. Though the group was cackling on like a coup full of chickens, Benny and Becca said nothing. They just stared off into the city.

As they passed the new bar on the corner of Union and Banks, Becca finally seemed to become aware of their vow of silence. "God, what time is it?" she groaned. "Did we seriously just walk that whole way and not say a word?" Benny, shaking himself from his stupor, looked at her and said, "I, uh… yep." With that, the two of them burst into laughter. Each had to maintain balance with something nearby. They laughed for a while, and their ability to speak returned to them. From that point into the next hour, there didn't seem to be a minute where they weren't talking. The two simply wandered the square, seemingly without breathing between words, and never stopping to sit or rest. They just wandered, laughed, and relaxed.

When their conversations had finally come to a casual halt, Benny realized they were standing in front of the theatre. He smiled and laughed to himself: "To think, I contemplated going to see a movie here tonight. If I'd done that, I'd have missed out on all the fun." Becca scoffed, "I really doubt you'd be worse off having missed tonight's action." The two stood there, looking at the employees inside still cleaning up the concession stand. "I'm sorry," Becca said, hanging her head finally. "I'm so sorry. This has been a living hell. I can't believe I put you through this." Benny turned to her. "What do you mean? You didn't do any of this. You were a captive too, remember?" Becca sighed, "I know, but you wouldn't have been through this were it not for me. I should never have brought this on you." Becca started to walk, but Benny stopped her, grabbing her by the wrist. "No," he said.

"I don't regret one bit of this." She looked at him with puzzlement. "But, why?" "Because," he said, a smile growing on his face, "this is the first time I've ever felt alive. Just a moment ago, a huge man was going to break my neck, and a crazed man was going to shoot us both. I was kidnapped, thrown in a van, told I was going to die, barely survived, and escaped with my life." She looked even more upset, but he only smiled even bigger. "I hit a guy with a golf cart, kicked a guy in the head, and rescued the girl. Becca, I wouldn't trade this night for anything in the world. You've shown me just how much I want to live. Thank you."

Becca smiled and said, "Well, I suppose that makes a little bit of sense. In that case, you're welcome for almost getting you killed." The two laughed and continued walking. Becca, after a good long laugh, yawned and said, "God, this has been exhausting. I'd offer to buy you some frozen yogurt were it not almost one thirty in the morning." Benny's eyes widened. "Good grief, is it really?" he said in shock. "God, I haven't called Karen. I bet she's freaking out." He started to reach for his phone, but he stopped himself. He could see something in Becca's face. What was it? He knew that look, but he couldn't put his finger on it.

The realization felt like a slap in the face. She was jealous. Becca was jealous of Karen. He could see that, and he withdrew his hand from his pocket. "You know, after this long, she can wait a little longer." Becca tried her best to not grin. "Well, listen pal, it's been fun, but I could really use some rest. Being kidnapped really takes it out of a girl," she mused, turning toward the northern end of the street. "How about you walk me home?" "My dear," he said in a terrible British accent while presenting his arm, "it would be a delight." The two laughed and walked toward Becca's apartment.

As they approached her stoop, Benny found himself wishing that they weren't parting ways. He wished that this wasn't clearly the end of their journey, that she wasn't going to become someone he once knew, someone he brought up in conversation when telling embarrassing stories with friends. She would, however, be a great story to remember, and he would love the years to come of talking about her. He tried to remind himself that the future was uncertain, that he couldn't possibly know what was going to happen from here, but he knew that wasn't true. The truth was simple: she was going to say good night, he would go home, and they'd slowly lose contact over time. She'd meet someone, he had Karen, and that would be it.

Trying to save face and not show it, Benny prepped himself for the good night and the good bye. As they walked to the door of her building, she turned with a small grin: "This is going to sound really stupid, but would you mind walking me to my apartment door? I'm a little shaken from tonight, and I don't know, I just..." He stopped her, saying, "My pleasure." She opened the door of her building, and they walked inside.

Her apartment building was built after the other buildings in the area had been around for years. A part of the city's renovation plans for the neighborhood, the complex had been constructed completely from the ground up, the previous building having been demolished due to mold. The walls were covered in the standard fare beige paint that apartment groups loved to use, and the halls were somehow bland and yet inviting. Becca's apartment was on the third floor, the same as Benny's, but her building had an elevator. Benny moved toward the elevator, but she turned instead to the stairs. "Don't be lazy on me now," she smirked, and the two climbed the two stories.

As they approached her door, Benny was at least glad that he had the chance to see her home. He had a chance to see her private life, albeit through the crack of a front door. This seemed like a rare opportunity, and he somehow felt special for being invited to experience it. She drew her key from her pocket to unlock the door, but then remarked, "Oh yeah, I was kidnapped," and pushed the door open. She turned her head to Benny and said, "Behold, my chambers." Benny grinned, "Seems like a nice place. Very homey." "Thanks," she said with a smile. "Decorated the place myself. Oh, and that's Cheddar." She pointed to a large orange and white blob on top of the couch. Hearing his own name, Cheddar uncurled himself and stretched, yawning. "Oh my, he's quite a tiger. Aren't you worried he'll run out the door?" Benny asked. She raised an eyebrow at him. "Honestly, look at him. Does he look like he runs anywhere?" They both chuckled. After a brief pause of watching Cheddar try to clean himself rather awkwardly and amusingly, Becca turned back to Benny.

"So, Ben, I guess this is the end of our date."

"Hey, since when was this a date?"

"Well, I think it really started when you and I left the frozen yogurt shop, but to be fair, you're the one that stared at me at the bridge."

"Wow, if I had known it was a date, I'd have knocked out our kidnappers sooner."

Becca laughed, placing a hand on his arm.

"Oh shut up. You had fun. I hope it wasn't too traumatizing."

"No, no, it was just traumatizing enough."

"Well good. I'll consider it a successful date then."

"Fair enough. I'd concede and call it a date as well."

"Oh good, then you'll come in, right?"

Benny paused with a choke. "I'm sorry, what?" Becca laughed: "Really? You're surprised? Look, we just went through something horrible and weird. I could use some company. You should definitely come in." Benny felt a lump rise in his throat. He wasn't breaking out into a flop sweat, but he sure felt like it. Was she asking him what he thought she was asking him? He must have said that out loud, because Becca grinned slyly and said, "Yes, that's what I'm saying. You really ought to come in."

Benny's heart was pounding. She was suggesting he come inside her apartment, stay for a while, and eventually have sex. He knew it, regardless of the large coy grin on her face. *What are you doing man? Get out of here. This is crazy. You have a girlfriend that you love and care about and would never hurt and oh God you totally want to sleep with her you horrible bastard what is wrong with you?* Benny choked back his heartbeat and tried to calm himself. "Becca, I,

uh," he stammered, searching for the polite way to say that he
wanted to sleep with her badly, but he was a committed man. She
laughed and said, "God, you are way too much fun to tease. Look,
it's okay. You're a good guy. I get that. Sorry if I'm totally turned
on by you." She patted him on the chest and smiled. "She's a
lucky lady. Make sure she knows it."

They said good night to each other several times in several
manners. Neither of them really knew how to end their interlude,
and eventually it became apparent that they could possibly stand
in the hall all night waiting for the other to say "Good bye."
Benny finally broke the ice with a comically exaggerated
handshake, she wrote her phone number on his hand with a
nearby pen, and they parted ways. He walked down the hall to
the elevator and jammed the button. The doors slid open, and he
entered the elevator car, slumping against the wall.

Outside her building, he was thankful that he couldn't see
her window from the street. He knew he'd look up to see if she
was there, and he was glad that he wouldn't have to lock eyes
with her and regret his decision. Benny was a good man. He
would never cheat on his girlfriend. She didn't deserve that. He
kept saying these things in his head, trying to push the desire out
of his mind to run back to her door and spend the night with her.
His mind raced with thoughts, both appropriate and
inappropriate, until he found himself standing at the front door
of his apartment complex.

He opened the door and walked into the stairwell that led to
his apartment. As he hit the first step, he suddenly realized that
he had never turned his phone back on after Demi turned it off.
Gosh, I bet Karen's called me twice already. I'll never hear the end of it, he
thought as he dug the phone from his pocket. Turning the device
back on, he held it in his hand as he climbed the stairs. After a
moment of booting up, the phone chimed with a new Voicemail
message, then another. And another. And another, and another,
and another. In total, the phone chimed thirteen times with
Voicemails.

Benny stopped. He dreaded the tone of her voice, hearing

her disdain in each Voicemail. She was probably worried sick and angry that he was ignoring her. She had never left so many messages before, but then again he couldn't remember the last time he'd gone this long without speaking to her. Dialing his Voicemail service, he checked the messages. "Hello. Please enter your pin." Benny punched the keys and put the phone back to his ear. "You have eighteen new voice mail messages."

"Eighteen?" Benny gasped aloud. Had she really called him eighteen times? This was going to get ugly quickly. He could already hear her yelling at him about how he was ignoring her. He had never, ever let her go that long without answering. He honestly couldn't even remember the last time he didn't answer her call immediately or call her right back within thirty seconds. Heaving a sigh of regret, he pressed the play key and awaited the onslaught of phone abuse.

The first message was about a minute long, and almost the entirety of the message consisted of rustling sounds and microphone scratches. She must have pocket dialed him by accident. He laughed to himself that he had worried so much about the call. Maybe she wasn't mad at all. He deleted the message and moved on.

The second message was more of the same sounds. This time, the call was ended with a sharp banging sound. Benny had to assume she'd pocket dialed again, and the phone had bumped into something. She was usually more responsible than this. She prided herself on never making "stupid, wasteful, air-headed calls." He would be sure to tease her about this later. With Message 3, Benny heard more sounds of rustling. Surely she hadn't made three of these calls. Now she was really going to hear about this. Finally, after a few moments, the call began. Karen was talking to someone. She was telling the person, judging from the depth of his voice to be a man, to stop doing that. She seemed to be giggling. She was teasing him, telling him that he shouldn't do that. Now she was saying things like, "Oh my" and "Oh God." Now she was moaning softly. *Wait. Did she just purr?* Benny couldn't be sure, but he knew one thing within the next few seconds: Karen was having sex. She was having sex with someone, and that someone was not Benny.

There was no question in his mind. Karen was cheating on him. The Voicemail message continued well into the act. Benny heard the moans and cries of his love, the love of his life, and he knew she was with another man. The man barely said a word, except for the occasional assumption that she hadn't ever had it this good and that she was a considerably "dirty girl." That only seemed to excite her more. The message abruptly ended moments before things presumably got even more heated.

Benny sat down on the step he was half-climbing. The message ended, and he did nothing. He couldn't move, he couldn't speak, and he couldn't push the button to delete the message. She cheated on him. He loved her, remained faithful, considered her the woman of his dreams, and she slept with another man. As if the fact needed declaration, Benny spoke the words out loud to himself. "She had sex with someone else." Benny felt his heart breaking. He was mortified. *How can she do this to me?* Benny pleaded with anyone in his mind that was listening.

Benny returned the phone to his ear, trying to decide if the Voicemail should be deleted. His Voicemail, however, had already moved on to the next message. The fourth message was very short, barely fifteen seconds. The time stamp indicated that the message had been left around thirty minutes later than the previous message. Karen had purposefully made the call this time.

"Hi sweetheart, it's me. Hey, did you call me? I can't tell. I think you might have tried to. I seem to have several calls from you, but you didn't leave me any messages. Is everything okay? You can call me back. I'll be free for a while. Kisses."

Benny was again left without words or feelings. She lied to him. She slept with another man, and then she lied to him. Sweetheart? Seriously? How did she have the nerve to even say that to him? How could she do that to him? He tried to bring himself to close the phone, but something drove him to listen to the rest of the messages.

"Message 5: 'Benny, is everything okay? Why haven't you called me back? You called me roughly forty minutes ago, didn't you? Let me check the time. (Benny heard the phone clicking from her nails against the screen) Yeah, I show here that you've called me three times. I don't under... wait. Oh, silly me. Those are calls where I've called you. But that doesn't make sense. I don't remember calling you then. I was busy. I guess I must have pocket dialed you by... oh... oh my... oh shit. Shit, shit, shit.' End of message."

"Message 6: 'Okay, I, um... I think I may have dialed you during... Listen, I'm not sure exactly when I called you, but I don't think I meant to. Did you hear anything? No, that's not what I mean. I mean... listen, I can explain... I mean, there's nothing to explain, because nothing happened. Just... uh... just call me back please. Love you.' End of message."

"Message 7: 'Shit, shit, shit. Okay, okay. I, um... I think you may have a Voicemail, and I'm assuming you've heard it already. Wow... this is going to be a hard one for me. Look, I didn't... I didn't do anything. Well, that's not... Listen, this has gotten out of hand. I just...' End of message."

"Message 8: 'You know what? Screw it. Yes, I had sex with someone. By now, you've heard the message, and you're pissed off at me. Well, I'll just tell you the truth: I had sex with someone. He's a coworker, and I've wanted him for a long time. We had sex, and I don't regret it. He was worth every second, and, God Almighty, is he good in bed. You can go to Hell. I don't give a damn what you think. I'm glad I did it.' End of message."

"Message 9: 'Oh Jesus, what have I done? Benny, wait, please. It's not like this. I made a huge mistake. I should never have done this. Oh God what have I done? I've ruined everything. I'm so damn stupid. I can't believe I've done this. (She begins crying).' End of message."

The calls continued in one long vicious repeating cycle, with Karen going from calling Benny the worst names he'd ever heard from her to begging his forgiveness and proclaiming that she was a pile of human refuse. Benny was mortified. He couldn't think of how to act or respond or even what level of anger he should feel. The messages played on, each worse than the last. One message was nothing but Karen sobbing and saying "stupid," "shit," and "Jesus," over and over again.

Benny felt the warm rush of pain coming to his face. He felt himself on the brink of tears. He leaned back against the railing of the stairs. He sighed and felt the water behind his eyes. Finally, he let go of the tension in his stomach. A snicker burst from his lips, and then a cough. And Benny began to laugh. He started with a gentle laugh, barely a chuckle. Soon, however, he was howling. With the last few messages, he barely heard what she was saying. He was in tears, laughing so hard he was gasping for breath.

The final message was supposed to be some kind of ultimatum for him, with Karen telling him about how miserable she'd been and what he had to do to win her affections. Benny barely listened at all, slamming the phone shut halfway through her diatribe. She had cheated on him, and he couldn't be happier. Suddenly, waves of relief, joy, sorrow, and elation all ran together in his mind. He was free, free from something he didn't even know he wanted to be free of until now.

He finally gathered himself, using the railing to pull himself up. He never expected this feeling, but he knew that he was done with her. He had found the escape from his empty relationship. In a way, his heart was broken, but only because of how unaware he had been in his misery. He began to climb the stairs, feeling the waves of grief and pain wash away. He was a new man. The whole night had given him such a new perspective on what was important. He now knew exactly what was missing in his life.

He reached the top of the stairs and turned to his door. Clutching his keys in his pocket, he drew them out to unlock his door. He wanted to share this feeling with someone, but he didn't know who would care. Kyle? Kyle wouldn't truly appreciate the feeling he had. His parents? Surely they'd rejoice, considering how much they reminded him that they didn't like Karen. Oh, maybe he could call Becca and tell…

Benny stopped. His mind raced back to the hall of Becca's apartment. He wanted to be near her, suddenly, and more than ever before. He needed to see her right then. Thrusting the keys into his pocket, Benny turned and dashed down the stairs, tripping on the second landing and catching himself just in time. As he reached the top of his stoop, he didn't even pause to catch the step. He vaulted from the top to the sidewalk. Pulling his coat tighter about him, he began to run down the sidewalk, setting his destination on Becca's front door.

Within minutes, he had reached her apartment building. Working his way up the stairs like a cheetah in pursuit of a gazelle, he bounded to the third floor and found himself looking down the hall to her front door. He checked his hair in the hall mirror, smiled at the joy on his face, took a moment to catch his breath, and walked to her door. The door was slightly cracked, having never been shut. *She must not shut her door all the way. That seems like her,* Benny chuckled to himself. *What should I do? Should I knock? I could just walk in. No, that might scare her. I'll just announce myself.*

Benny dusted the front of his coat off and took a deep breath. He put his hand on the door and pressed gently, saying, "You know, I just remembered that I left something here. I should totally come in and get that something." He cracked a huge smile, gleefully awaiting the sight of her surprised face. Pushing the door further open, he strode into the living room and met the surprised face of Becca. Becca seemed distracted at the moment, probably because she wasn't alone. Standing across from her, his clothes somewhat glued to him and hardened by dried liquid adhesive, stood Demi with a horrible grimace and his pistol raised. Caught by surprise, Demi turned his attention to Benny. As if by instinct, Benny turned and grabbed the closest thing to him: a thin, rolled and fastened umbrella. Turning his eyes to Demi, he hurled the umbrella like a spear towards Demi's head. Demi swung his arm and fired right as the umbrella hit him in the head. Curling his body and reeling from the pain of the attack, Demi never saw Becca as she grabbed a nearby free-weight and struck Demi in the head, knocking him unconscious.

Becca knelt down, checking to be sure Demi was out cold. Suddenly, her awareness returned to her, and she looked to Benny. Benny was down on his knees, clutching his chest. As he fell to his side, Becca rushed to his side, shouting, "No, Ben. No, no, no Ben, no God please no." Benny didn't answer. She pulled his hand away to find his coat stained with a small blob of blood. Pulling the coat back, she saw a growing red stain blotched against his shirt. "Oh God, no, no," Becca cried, grabbing her phone. Benny put a hand out onto hers and strained a half-cocked smile. "Hey there, good lookin' trouble," he whispered through strained breaths. His hand fell limp, and he closed his eyes.

CHAPTER FOURTEEN

Becca stood in the middle bedroom of Ben's empty two-bedroom apartment. The bed, the dressers, and the other smaller pieces of furniture were loaded in the truck. All that remained was a proper good bye. As she walked through the apartment, she wondered about all the stories she might have missed. Having never spent any time there, at least not in the year and a half that he had lived there, she couldn't help but to wish she'd been a part of his life. She wondered what he had done, whom he'd spent his time with, and if he'd at least had fun here. His stories had never really been about this place.

She wandered into the extra room and leaned against the door frame. The walls were almost perfect, barely scarred by any marks or holes. He clearly never spent any time in this room. The only coloration of the room was a small white stain on the floor. From the looks of it, he'd had to clean something up, but it hadn't come up completely. Becca speculated that it was bird poop, but she couldn't figure out why a bird would have been in here long enough to do that.

Turning back to the hallway leading past the kitchen, she walked along, running her hands against the walls. She yearned to talk to the walls, to learn their secrets about him. What had they seen? Could they tell her more about what he was like? She wanted to know so much about him, to really know his deepest secrets. She laughed, thinking back to how she'd found the fridge barren except for the half-jug of orange juice and the single can of disgusting, cheap beer. She marveled at how he could possibly have so little in his home and yet still find joy somehow.

The halls had a kind of homey smell to them, and she found herself led through the rooms like touring a great museum. She made her way to the living room and looked out the glass of the French doors leading to the balcony. She had never gotten to truly enjoy sitting on the balcony, watching the sun as it set over the city. Though she feared letting out all the interesting odors of the old apartment, she opened the doors of the balcony and walked out onto the tile floor.

The city was somewhat quiet, though the city never really had a moment of silence. The view was truly spectacular, and she wondered if that was the reason he had ever signed the lease to begin with. Looking out over the city at the midday sun, she wished they'd had just one night there together, watching the stars come alive against the night sky. She wished for a lot of things with him, but she would have settled for that one night together.

Gathering her composure, she looked around the apartment for any remaining items and then placed the key by the front door's shelf. Closing the front door behind her, she descended the stairs and made her way outside to the moving truck. As she reached the street, she knew that the time was coming to say goodbye for good. She'd been dreading it all day, but she had to face the truth at some point. The past few months had been the best she'd ever known, and she would always treasure them. *All good things must come to an end. Or something like that. I just wish I'd had more time with him.*

A loud crashing sound within the back of the truck interrupted her moment of solemn reflection. She ran to the edge of the bed and looked up into the back. "What the hell did you do now?" she asked. Ben looked up from the pile of boxes he'd collapsed onto and said, "Woah, woah, don't look at me. You're the one that packed this section. This was totally not my fault. Definitely not." "Uh huh, sure," she replied, laughing over his messed up hair and dirty face. Sometimes, she really hated how handsome he was.

After gathering himself, he stepped to the edge of the truck bed. "Thanks again for all your help. I never would have gotten this thing packed by myself." She put her hands to her hips and sighed with relief. "Well, you know, someone had to be here to do all the heavy lifting." He sighed and rolled his eyes. "Yes, you're a walking powerhouse. No box is too heavy for your arm cannons." He jumped down to the ground, stumbling a little upon landing. She tried to hide her laughter.

The two stood in the street, studying the back of the truck. "I think that's everything," he said, wiping his brow. Did we forget anything?" "I didn't see anything back in your apartment," she replied. "Can you think of anything you've forgotten to pack?" He paused for a moment and then said, "No, that should be it." She smiled, "Well good. You're ready to go then." He turned and reached up to the truck door, pulling the rolling door down and latching it. "And now the ramp," he said, lifting the ramp and sliding it into place beneath the back lip. "Well go on, hit the road," she said, trying to seem tough and aloof. "You should probably get going before it gets too late."

Ben stood there, studying the back of the truck. "Yeah," he said after a pause, "I guess so." He looked around the truck, checking more places, but Becca soon realized that there wasn't anything for him to check any further. "Is something wrong?" she asked. He stopped and looked at her. "No, no, everything's fine. I'm just worried I'll forget something," he said. "Well," she quizzed, "can you think of anything you're forgetting to take?" He looked at her and smiled.

She studied his face for a moment. "What?" she asked. He simply smiled at her. Finally, her eyes widened. "Do you... do you want me to come with you?" "Why not?" he replied. "I could use a moving companion, and I'll probably need a roommate when I get to my place. If nothing else, it gets you out of this town." She felt her face turning red as the rush of panic, excitement, fear, and pure joy washed over her. "This is crazy," she mumbled. "We barely know each other. I mean, I met you five months ago." "So?" Ben replied. "You have something here worth staying for? You're gonna wait for your ex-boyfriend and his idiot brother to get out of jail? Need I remind you that he shot me?" Ben patted his chest around the almost-healed wound. "No, of course not," she scoffed, rolling her eyes. "It's just that this isn't the kind of decision people make on a whim. You're off to live your life, and I'm off to live mine. How could we ever-" but she cut herself off. Looking into his eyes, she began to smile. "Oh screw it. I'm in. Let's get the hell out of here," she sighed. From up above them, Mrs. Meinher let out a cheer. "Finally! It's about time you two did something right." Ben looked up at her and sighed. "How long have you been there?" he asked. "Long enough to watch you two dance around this whole damn thing," she shouted down. "You two kids belong together. Now shut up and get going."

Ben turned to Becca and said, "You heard the lady. Let's head over to your place and start packing some things." She began to grin wildly and rushed away to hide her face. As she hopped into the front seat of the truck, Ben looked up and Mrs. Meinher and said, "So, what do you think? Am I still a -- what's that word you use -- a schmuck?" She looked down at him with loving eyes and said, "My boy, you're gonna be a schmuck until the day you die, and that's what makes you so loveable. Take good care of yourself, Benjamin." He smiled, feeling a few tears come to his eyes. "You too, Mrs. Meinher. Thanks for everything." With that, he walked to the truck and opened the front cab door. He knew that Becca was sitting there, but he still felt the excitement upon seeing her in the seat.

Stepping up into the truck, he sat down next to her. "I'm really glad you're coming with me." She grinned and said, "Shut up. I'm going because I want to move. It has nothing to do with you. No way, no how." He laughed and said, "Okay, whatever you have to tell yourself. You've got it bad for me. We both know it." She scoffed. "Is that so? Seems like you're the one that invited me on this adventure." "Well, yeah," he replied. "How am I supposed to go on without you?" She rolled her eyes with a smile. "Damn you," she said, and grabbed him by the shirt, pulling him into a long, passionate kiss. The kiss lasted far longer than either expected. Finally, the two pulled away, each dazed by the expression. "We've waited way too long to do that," he said. "God, that's the truth. Now, drive," she replied.

Ben laughed and put the key into the ignition. He turned the key, but nothing happened. "Well that's not good," he replied, studying the dash of the truck. "We can't possibly be out of gas, and I know the battery isn't dead." Becca laughed, "Are you sure you know how to drive this thing?" "Of course," he said. "I just need to make sure that... um..." He stopped mid-sentence and paused. Pressing down on the clutch, he turned the key again and felt the truck engine come to life. "Really?" she asked. "I don't want to talk about it," he said, keeping his eyes on the road. They pulled out into the street and made their way down to the corner. As they reached the corner of the block, Ben's phone began to ring. He dug into his pocket and fished the phone out. "Oh come on, you can't be serious," he said, throwing his head back against the headrest. "Is it really her calling again?" Becca asked. "This is insane. What could we possibly talk about? There's nothing left to say," he replied. Rolling the truck window down. "What are you going to do?" Becca asked, leaning forward to watch him. "Something I've always wanted to do," he said, and with that, he threw the phone as hard as he could across the street into the nearby brick wall. The phone slammed into the brick and shattered into countless pieces. "I can't believe you just did that," she gasped. "That was awesome." "Eh," he replied with a shrug, "I'll get another phone." As they pulled away, the phone's speaker crackled the ringtone one last time before falling silent. The call had gone to Voicemail.

As they pulled up in front of Becca's building, she turned to Ben and asked, "Are you sure you want to do this?" "I've never been surer of anything in my life," he replied. She kissed him again, and opened the door of the truck. "Well then come up stairs with me, please," she said, winking at him. "I believe I'll need some help packing my things." With that, she turned and ran up the stairs. He grinned like an idiot, watching her run away into her building. He turned off the truck and stepped out, closing the door firmly behind him. The sun was just beginning to come out from behind the high rises of the city, and he took a moment to pause, feeling the warm light on his face. "Now, this," he said aloud to himself with a sigh, "This is living."

With that, he turned and walked toward her building. Stepping up onto the sidewalk from the street, he began whistling to himself while tossing the keys in the air. As he looked up at the keys, his foot caught a small crack in the side walk, and he tripped. The keys came down on his head, striking him with the pointed tips down. "Ow," he cried out, catching the keys as they fell into his hand. He looked around to see if anyone saw him, grumbled to himself, and hurried inside.

ABOUT THE AUTHOR

Ryan Spargo has spent almost all of his life never shutting up, so it's rather fitting that he decided to become a storyteller. This is his first novel, so you'll have to forgive him for doting over it like a new father. When he isn't writing and telling stories, he's laughing, singing, talking to himself, and creating other ways to bother people with his stories. He is married to a wonderful woman (you'd know that if you had read the Acknowledgments) and lives in Tennessee, though it's hard to keep his feet on the ground. Or his mouth shut. Did I mention he talks a lot?

33239466R00092

Made in the USA
Middletown, DE
05 July 2016